# India " Unity lies in Diversity"

Swatantra Bahadur and Mahima Tripathi

Published by Swatantra Bahadur, 2023.

INDIA " UNITY LIES IN DIVERSITY"

**First edition. September 26, 2023.**

Copyright © 2023 Swatantra Bahadur and Mahima Tripathi.

ISBN: 979-8223969037

Written by Swatantra Bahadur and Mahima Tripathi.

# Disclaimer

The information presented in this book is intended for general informational purposes only and should not be relied upon as a substitute for professional advice or judgment. The author and publisher are not responsible for any action taken by readers based on the information provided in this book. Readers should seek appropriate professional advice or conduct their own research before making decisions related to the topics discussed in this book. The views expressed in this book are those of the author and do not necessarily reflect the views of the publisher.

# Contents

I. Introduction
A. Brief explanation of the concept of "Unity in Diversity"
B. Significance of "Unity in Diversity" in the context of India
C. Purpose of the outline
II. Historical Background
A. Diversity of cultures, languages, and religions in ancient India
B. Key empires and rulers that contributed to India's diversity
C. Early examples of unity despite diversity
III. Cultural Diversity
A. Overview of India's diverse cultural heritage
B. Regional variations in food, clothing, and traditions
C. The role of festivals in celebrating diversity
IV. Linguistic Diversity
A. The multitude of languages spoken in India
B. Importance of preserving and promoting linguistic diversity
C. The role of Hindi and English as link languages
V. Religious Diversity
A. Major religions in India (Hinduism, Islam, Christianity, Sikhism, Buddhism, Jainism, etc.)
B. Interactions and coexistence of various religious communities
C. Religious tolerance and secularism in the Indian Constitution
VI. Social and Ethnic Diversity
A. Caste system and its impact on social diversity

B. Tribal communities and their unique cultural practices

C. Efforts to promote social inclusivity and equality

VII. Political Unity

A. India's struggle for independence and the role of unity in diversity

B. Formation of the Indian Union and its diverse states

C. Challenges in maintaining political unity

VIII. Economic Diversity

A. Regional variations in economic development

B. Contribution of different regions to India's economy

C. Government policies to address economic disparities

IX. Challenges to Unity in Diversity

A. Communal tensions and religious conflicts

B. Caste-based discrimination and social inequality

C. Regional disparities and separatist movements

X. Measures to Promote Unity in Diversity

A. Educational initiatives to foster tolerance and inclusivity

B. Government policies to promote cultural exchange and understanding

C. Grassroots efforts to bridge divides

XI. Conclusion

A. Reiteration of the importance of "Unity in Diversity" in India

B. Reflection on India's potential as a role model for the world

C. Call to embrace and celebrate diversity while striving for unity

# Introduction

India, often hailed as the world's largest democracy and a land of myriad traditions, languages, religions, and cultures, exemplifies the profound adage, "Unity lies in diversity." This phrase encapsulates the essence of a nation that stands as a testament to the harmonious coexistence of a kaleidoscope of identities and beliefs within its borders. The diverse tapestry of India, woven together by the threads of tolerance, inclusivity, and shared aspirations, serves as a shining example to the world.

In this discourse, we embark on a journey to explore the deep-rooted concept of unity in diversity within the Indian context. We will delve into the historical, cultural, religious, and social dimensions of India's diversity and investigate the threads that have bound this nation together through millennia. From ancient empires to modern democratic principles, from languages that span the spectrum of human speech to a tapestry of faiths and practices, India's story is one of resilience, adaptation, and unity amidst multiplicity.

As we navigate through the intricacies of India's diversity, we will also confront the challenges it faces, such as communal tensions, caste-based disparities, and regional differences. Through this exploration, we aim not only to understand the concept of unity in diversity but also to appreciate its significance, offering valuable insights into how a nation can thrive when it embraces its differences while nurturing a common bond. Ultimately, India's journey embodies a powerful message: that unity can indeed flourish amidst the beautiful tapestry of diversity, and in doing so, it can inspire the world.

# A. Brief Explanation of the Concept of "Unity in Diversity"

The concept of "Unity in Diversity" is a philosophical and sociocultural idea that emphasizes the coexistence of different cultures, religions, languages, and ethnicities within a single community or nation while maintaining a sense of unity, harmony, and shared identity. It underscores the idea that diversity is not a source of division but rather a source of strength, enrichment, and collective progress.

In the context of India, "Unity in Diversity" embodies the idea that despite its vast and varied cultural, linguistic, and religious landscape, the nation remains united as one entity. It recognizes that India's diversity is not a hindrance to its unity but rather the very foundation upon which the nation's unity is built. This concept reflects the inclusive ethos of Indian society, where people from different backgrounds coexist, respect each other's differences, and contribute to the tapestry of the nation's identity.

"Unity in Diversity" celebrates the idea that a nation can draw strength from the multiplicity of its people and their unique traditions, rather than seeking homogeneity. It promotes tolerance, multiculturalism, and social cohesion, advocating for the equitable treatment of all citizens, regardless of their cultural or religious affiliations.

Throughout history, India has exemplified this concept, serving as a living testament to the possibility of harmonious coexistence amid diversity. It is a concept that not only defines India but also resonates with societies around the world striving to create inclusive and harmonious nations.

# B. Significance of "Unity in Diversity" in the Context of India

Cultural Heritage Preservation:

India's vast cultural diversity, comprising numerous languages, traditions, art forms, and cuisines, is a testament to the country's rich history.

"Unity in Diversity" signifies India's commitment to preserving and celebrating this cultural heritage, ensuring that unique traditions are passed down through generations.

Social Harmony:

In a country as diverse as India, social harmony is crucial for peaceful coexistence.

The concept underscores the significance of respecting and embracing differences, reducing social tensions, and promoting mutual understanding among communities.

National Identity:

India's unity in diversity forms the core of its national identity. It recognizes that every Indian, regardless of their background, is an integral part of the nation.

This concept helps foster a sense of belonging and pride among Indians, reinforcing their shared identity as citizens of a diverse yet united country.

Global Example:

India's success in maintaining unity amidst diversity serves as an inspiring example for the world.

In an era marked by cultural clashes and ethnic conflicts, India's model of coexistence and tolerance offers a beacon of hope, demonstrating that diversity can be a source of strength rather than division.

Economic Advancement:

India's diverse regions contribute differently to its economic development.

"Unity in Diversity" encourages the equitable distribution of resources and opportunities, ensuring that every part of the country plays a role in its economic growth.

Political Stability:

The concept plays a vital role in India's political stability by promoting inclusive governance.

India's democratic system accommodates the interests of diverse groups, facilitating political stability and avoiding polarization.

Soft Power:

India's cultural diversity, expressed through art, music, dance, and literature, contributes to its soft power on the global stage.

The concept of unity in diversity enhances India's influence, as it showcases the nation's ability to balance tradition and modernity.

Tolerance and Secularism:

"Unity in Diversity" is closely tied to India's constitutional commitment to secularism and religious tolerance.

This commitment ensures that all religions and belief systems are respected and protected, contributing to the nation's social fabric.

In summary, "Unity in Diversity" is not just a slogan in India; it is a guiding principle that shapes the nation's identity, values, and policies. It highlights the significance of embracing differences, fostering social harmony, and ensuring that all citizens have an equal stake in the nation's progress, making it a foundational concept in the Indian ethos.

# C. Purpose of the Book "India: Unity Lies in Diversity"

Educational Insight: The primary purpose of this book is to provide readers with a comprehensive understanding of the concept of "Unity in Diversity" as it manifests in the context of India. It aims to educate and inform by delving deep into the historical, cultural, religious, and social aspects of India's diversity, and how this diversity has contributed to the nation's unity.

Promotion of Tolerance and Inclusivity: The book seeks to promote values of tolerance, inclusivity, and social cohesion. It highlights the importance of respecting differences and fostering an environment where diverse communities coexist harmoniously.

Historical Context: By exploring India's historical background, the book aims to shed light on how the concept of unity amid diversity has evolved over centuries. It demonstrates how India's diverse past has shaped its present identity.

Contemporary Relevance: The book aims to show the contemporary relevance of "Unity in Diversity" in India. It discusses the challenges faced by the nation in maintaining this unity and offers insights into how these challenges can be addressed in the modern context.

Cultural Appreciation: It serves as a platform to celebrate India's cultural richness and diversity, showcasing various traditions, languages, art forms, and cuisines from different parts of the country. It invites readers to appreciate the beauty of India's cultural tapestry.

National Identity: The book emphasizes the role of unity in diversity in shaping India's national identity. It aims to instill a sense of pride and belonging among Indians by reinforcing that every citizen, regardless of their background, contributes to the nation's unique identity.

Global Perspective: In a globalized world, where diversity is increasingly important, the book positions India as a global example of how diverse communities can coexist and thrive. It encourages readers to reflect on the broader implications of unity in diversity.

Policy Insights: The book may offer insights for policymakers on how to address issues related to diversity, inclusivity, and social harmony in India. It could serve as a resource for those interested in crafting policies that promote unity amid diversity.

Inspiration: Ultimately, the book aims to inspire readers, both within and beyond India, by demonstrating that unity in diversity is not just an ideal but a practical and sustainable way for a nation to progress. It invites readers to consider how similar principles might be applied in their own contexts.

In summary, "India: Unity Lies in Diversity" is a book with a multifaceted purpose, ranging from education and cultural celebration to promoting values of tolerance and inclusivity. It aims to explore the concept deeply, offering historical insights and contemporary relevance, and serves as a guide for individuals, policymakers, and anyone interested in understanding how diversity can be a source of strength and unity.

# II. Historical Background

The timeless adage "Unity in Diversity" finds no more profound and vibrant embodiment than in the vast and storied subcontinent of India. To truly grasp the essence of India's unity amid its astonishing diversity, one must embark on a journey through the annals of its history. For it is within the pages of India's past that the threads of this enduring concept are intricately woven, shaping the nation's identity, values, and very soul.

India's historical tapestry is marked by an unparalleled mosaic of cultures, languages, religions, and civilizations. From the ancient Indus Valley to the mighty Maurya and Gupta empires, from the arrival of Buddhism to the spread of Islam, India's history is a testament to the ebb and flow of human migrations and ideas. Throughout the centuries, it has been the crucible where myriad influences converged, intermingled, and, in their diversity, found a unique unity.

In this exploration of India's historical background, we will journey through the ages, tracing the roots of unity in diversity from its earliest manifestations to its modern-day significance. We will discover how empires such as the Mauryas and the Mughals fostered cultural exchange and religious syncretism, and how the Indian subcontinent became a melting pot of ideas, languages, and traditions.

The historical context also reveals how the concept of unity in diversity was championed by remarkable leaders like Mahatma Gandhi, who envisioned a unified, independent India that would respect and honor its diversity. The struggle for independence from British colonial rule, marked by a diverse coalition of leaders and activists, showcased the power of unity forged amidst differences.

As we embark on this historical journey, we will encounter the intersections of cultures, the coexistence of religions, and the preservation of traditions that have contributed to India's unique identity. We will also confront the challenges and conflicts that have arisen along the way, underscoring the constant need for nurturing unity while respecting diversity.

In tracing India's historical background, we will come to appreciate that "Unity in Diversity" is not merely a modern catchphrase but an enduring and integral part of India's DNA. It is a principle that has not only shaped the nation but also served as an enduring source of inspiration for the world, demonstrating that from the crucible of diversity can emerge the unbreakable bonds of unity.

# A. Diversity of Cultures, Languages, and Religions in Ancient India

Cultural Diversity:

Ancient India was a tapestry of diverse cultures, each with its unique customs, traditions, and practices.

The Indus Valley Civilization (circa 3300–1300 BCE) showcased early examples of urban culture, advanced architecture, and a system of writing.

Linguistic Diversity:

Ancient India was a linguistic marvel with a plethora of languages spoken across its regions.

The ancient Sanskrit language served as a unifying force for intellectual and religious discourse, giving rise to classical literature like the Vedas and epics like the Mahabharata and Ramayana.

Religious Pluralism:

Ancient India was a fertile ground for religious diversity and the birthplace of several major religions.

Hinduism, one of the world's oldest religions, evolved over thousands of years and absorbed various regional beliefs and practices.

Buddhism, founded by Siddhartha Gautama (Buddha), emerged in India around the 6th century BCE and spread across Asia.

Jainism, with its emphasis on non-violence and asceticism, also originated in ancient India.

The arrival of Islam in the 7th century CE introduced a new religious dimension, leading to the coexistence of multiple faiths.

Regional Distinctiveness:

India's vast geographical expanse contributed to regional diversity in customs and traditions.

The Dravidian culture of South India differed from the Aryan-influenced culture of North India, giving rise to distinctive languages, art forms, and cuisines.

Trade and Cultural Exchange:

Ancient India was a hub for trade and cultural exchange, leading to the assimilation of foreign influences.

The Silk Road facilitated the exchange of goods and ideas with neighboring regions, enriching Indian culture.

Cultural Achievements:

India's cultural diversity fostered remarkable achievements in art, architecture, literature, and philosophy.

The temples of Khajuraho, the intricate carvings of Ellora and Ajanta, and the monumental stupa at Sanchi stand as testaments to ancient India's artistic prowess.

Religious Tolerance:

Ancient India was characterized by religious tolerance, where different faiths coexisted and often influenced each other.

The teachings of ancient Indian philosophers and scholars emphasized respect for diverse religious beliefs.

In summary, ancient India was a melting pot of cultures, languages, and religions. Its rich diversity, rather than being a source of division, served as a foundation for the country's cultural and spiritual growth. This legacy of embracing diversity has continued to shape India's identity, making "Unity in Diversity" not just a contemporary ideal but a time-honored tradition.

# B. Key Empires and Rulers that Contributed to India's Diversity

Maurya Empire (c. 322–185 BCE):

Emperor Ashoka, one of the most significant rulers of the Maurya Dynasty, embraced Buddhism and promoted religious tolerance through his inscriptions and edicts.

His reign marked an era of inclusivity and cultural diversity, as Buddhism spread not only within India but also to other parts of Asia.

Gupta Empire (c. 320–550 CE):

The Gupta Empire is often referred to as the "Golden Age" of India, during which art, science, and culture flourished.

Rulers like Chandragupta II and Samudragupta supported various religious traditions, including Hinduism, Buddhism, and Jainism.

This period witnessed the compilation of the great Sanskrit epics, the Ramayana and Mahabharata, and the development of classical Indian art forms.

Mughal Empire (c. 1526–1857):

The Mughal Empire, established by Babur, embraced religious pluralism and cultural syncretism.

Akbar the Great, in particular, promoted religious tolerance through policies like the Din-i Ilahi, a syncretic religion that aimed to bridge the gaps between different faiths.

The Mughal era saw a fusion of Persian, Islamic, and Indian architectural styles, exemplified by iconic monuments like the Taj Mahal.

Chola Dynasty (c. 9th–13th centuries):

The Chola Dynasty in South India encouraged the development of Dravidian culture and languages.

Their reign witnessed a flowering of art, temple architecture, and literature in Tamil.

Sultanate of Delhi (c. 13th–16th centuries):

While the Delhi Sultanate was initially marked by Islamic rule, it also saw the convergence of diverse cultures through trade and diplomacy.

Sufi saints played a pivotal role in fostering interfaith dialogue and tolerance.

Vijayanagara Empire (c. 14th–17th centuries):

The Vijayanagara Empire in South India celebrated Hinduism but also displayed a remarkable degree of religious inclusivity.

Temples like the Vitthala Temple in Hampi showcased the fusion of various architectural styles.

British Raj (c. 1858–1947):

The British colonial period witnessed the confluence of Indian and Western cultures.

The spread of English language, education, and the introduction of Western institutions had a profound impact on Indian society, shaping its modern diversity.

These empires and rulers left an indelible mark on India's history, not only by governing vast territories but also by fostering an environment of cultural exchange and religious harmony. Their contributions to India's diversity continue to influence the nation's identity and its commitment to the concept of "Unity in Diversity."

# C. Early examples of unity despite diversity

India, with its ancient civilization dating back millennia, offers profound historical examples of unity in the face of remarkable diversity. These early instances showcase the nation's ability to harness its pluralistic character as a source of strength and harmony. Here are some prominent examples:

1. Mauryan Empire (c. 322–185 BCE):

● Under the reign of Emperor Ashoka, the Mauryan Empire saw the coexistence of various religious traditions, including Hinduism, Buddhism, and Jainism.

● Ashoka's rock edicts emphasized tolerance and moral principles, promoting social harmony and unity among diverse religious communities.

2. Buddhism's Spread:

● Buddhism, founded in India by Siddhartha Gautama (Buddha), transcended caste and cultural boundaries.

● It gained followers from various backgrounds, emphasizing universal truths and the path to enlightenment, fostering unity among its practitioners.

3. The Great Emperor Akbar (1542–1605):

● Akbar, one of the Mughal Empire's most renowned rulers, promoted religious tolerance through policies like "Sulh-e-Kul" (peace with all).

● He held discussions with scholars of various religions, fostering interfaith dialogue and understanding.

4. Harmony in the Indian Epics:

● The ancient Indian epics, the Mahabharata and Ramayana, narrate stories of unity and cooperation despite diversity.

● Characters from diverse backgrounds, beliefs, and regions come together to confront challenges, emphasizing shared values and virtues.

5. The Syncretic Architecture of India:

● India's architectural heritage, such as the Ellora Caves and Khajuraho Temples, showcases the fusion of diverse cultural and religious influences.

● These sites feature Hindu, Jain, and Buddhist temples in close proximity, symbolizing religious unity within architectural diversity.

6. Diversity in Language and Literature:

• India's linguistic diversity has been celebrated through its classical languages and literature, such as Sanskrit, Tamil, and Pali.

• Scholars from various linguistic backgrounds contributed to the creation and preservation of knowledge, demonstrating unity in cultural diversity.

7. Ashramas and Gurukulas:

• Ancient India's education system, with its ashramas and gurukulas, welcomed students from various social and religious backgrounds.

• Scholars and students engaged in dialogue and the exchange of knowledge, fostering intellectual unity.

8. Trade and Cultural Exchange:

• India's position on the Silk Road facilitated the exchange of goods and ideas with neighboring regions.

• This trade and cultural interaction allowed for the assimilation of diverse influences while maintaining India's own unique identity.

• These early examples illustrate India's deep-rooted commitment to unity despite diversity, demonstrating that the nation's ability to embrace differences while emphasizing shared values has been a hallmark of its cultural and historical legacy. Such instances continue to inspire India's modern ethos, reinforcing the enduring truth that diversity can be a source of strength and unity.

# III. Religious Diversity in India

India, the land of spirituality and ancient wisdom, stands as a radiant example of how religious diversity can be a wellspring of unity rather than division. With a kaleidoscope of faiths, beliefs, and practices, India is a living testament to the profound concept that "Unity Lies in Diversity." Its religious landscape is a captivating mosaic, where countless paths to the divine coexist, fostering a harmonious tapestry of spiritual devotion and communal harmony.

In this exploration of religious diversity in India, we embark on a journey through the centuries, tracing the origins and evolution of its major religions. From the birthplace of Hinduism, Buddhism, and Jainism to the spread of Islam, Christianity, Sikhism, and myriad indigenous belief systems, India's spiritual history is a complex web of interactions, syncretism, and coexistence.

The significance of religious diversity in India extends far beyond matters of faith alone. It is deeply ingrained in the country's social fabric, cultural heritage, and even its political identity. Over millennia, India has embraced an ethos of tolerance, respect, and acceptance, where diverse religious communities have found both sanctuary and the freedom to flourish.

In this context, we will delve into the multifaceted aspects of religious diversity in India. We will explore the coexistence of temples, mosques, gurdwaras, churches, and monasteries, often side by side, in a display of unity amid difference. We will examine the rituals, festivals, and traditions that bring people of various faiths together, forging bonds that transcend religious boundaries.

Religious diversity in India is not without its challenges and complexities, from historical conflicts to contemporary issues. But it is precisely in these complexities that the nation's commitment to unity shines most brightly. Through dialogue, interfaith initiatives, and constitutional safeguards, India continues to navigate the delicate balance between the plurality of beliefs and the unity of its people.

Ultimately, India's religious diversity is a source of strength, an embodiment of the enduring idea that, in this land of myriad gods and diverse paths, unity thrives. It is a testament to the coexistence of spiritual aspirations and communal cohesion, reminding the world that the pursuit of divinity can walk hand in hand with the celebration of differences. In exploring India's religious diversity, we seek not only to understand but also to celebrate the remarkable tapestry of faiths that together proclaim that "Unity Lies in Diversity."

# A. Overview of India's Diverse Cultural Heritage

India's cultural heritage is a treasure trove of diversity, reflecting thousands of years of history, influences, and traditions. This overview highlights the rich tapestry of India's cultural heritage:

Ancient Roots:

India's cultural heritage dates back to one of the world's oldest known civilizations, the Indus Valley Civilization, which thrived around 3300–1300 BCE.

The Vedas, ancient texts that form the foundation of Hinduism, represent some of the earliest literary and philosophical contributions.

Religious Diversity:

India is the birthplace of major religions like Hinduism, Buddhism, Jainism, and Sikhism. It is also home to thriving communities of Muslims, Christians, Jews, Zoroastrians, and others.

This diversity is reflected in religious practices, festivals, and architectural marvels like temples, mosques, churches, and gurdwaras that dot the landscape.

Languages and Linguistic Diversity:

India is a linguistic mosaic, with over 19,000 languages and dialects spoken across the country.

The constitution recognizes 22 officially recognized languages, with Hindi and English serving as official languages at the national level.

Art and Architecture:

India boasts a stunning array of architectural marvels, from ancient temples like the temples of Khajuraho and Konark to the grandeur of Mughal architecture represented by the Taj Mahal.

Traditional art forms such as Bharatanatyam, Kathak, Odissi, and classical music like Hindustani and Carnatic are integral to India's cultural heritage.

Cuisine and Culinary Diversity:

Indian cuisine is celebrated for its diversity, with each region offering distinct flavors, ingredients, and cooking techniques.

Staple ingredients like rice, wheat, lentils, and spices are used creatively to create a vast array of dishes.

Traditional Clothing and Textiles:

Traditional clothing varies widely across regions, with attire like sarees, dhotis, turbans, and sherwanis being deeply rooted in cultural identity.

India's textile industry is known for its intricate craftsmanship, with each region producing unique fabrics and embroidery styles.

Festivals and Celebrations:

Festivals like Diwali, Holi, Eid, Christmas, Durga Puja, and Navratri showcase the vibrant colors, music, dance, and traditions of India.

These celebrations unite people from diverse backgrounds in shared joy and reverence.

Ancient Knowledge Systems:

India's contributions to mathematics, astronomy, medicine, and philosophy have had a profound impact on global knowledge systems.

Scholars like Aryabhata, Sushruta, and Panini made pioneering contributions that continue to influence modern science and thought.

Traditional Practices and Yoga:

Ancient practices like yoga and Ayurveda originated in India and continue to be practiced worldwide for their holistic health benefits.

Yoga, in particular, has transcended cultural boundaries to become a global wellness phenomenon.

Cultural Exchange:

India's strategic location on trade routes facilitated cultural exchange with neighboring regions, leading to the assimilation of diverse influences.

In essence, India's cultural heritage is a vibrant amalgamation of ancient wisdom, artistic excellence, religious pluralism, and a profound appreciation for diversity. It continues to evolve, celebrating both its historical roots and its role in shaping a dynamic, modern nation. India's cultural richness serves as a source of pride and inspiration, resonating with people from all corners of the globe.

# B. Regional Variations in Food, Clothing, and Traditions in India

India's vast geographical expanse and diverse cultural landscape give rise to remarkable regional variations in food, clothing, and traditions. These variations are a testament to the country's multicultural richness. Here is an overview of the regional diversity in India:

Food:

North India:

North Indian cuisine is known for its use of dairy products like ghee and yogurt, as well as wheat-based bread such as roti and naan.

Signature dishes include biryani, kebabs, tandoori chicken, and various types of paneer (Indian cheese) dishes.

Sweets like gulab jamun and jalebi are popular, and chai (spiced tea) is a beloved beverage.

South India:

South Indian cuisine prominently features rice, coconut, and an array of spices.

Dishes like dosa, idli, sambar, and rasam are staples, often served with coconut chutneys.

South India is also famous for its filter coffee and a wide variety of sweets, including Mysore pak.

East India:

The cuisine of East India showcases a mix of fish, rice, and mustard oil, with a range of vegetarian and non-vegetarian options.

Dishes like macher jhol (fish curry), sandesh (sweet), and various street foods are unique to the region.

West India:

West Indian cuisine boasts a diverse range of flavors, with a preference for spicy and tangy dishes.

Popular items include dhokla, pav bhaji, vada pav, and the legendary Gujarati thali.

Sweets like shrikhand and modak are delightful treats from this region.

Clothing:

North India:

Traditional clothing in North India includes attire like sarees for women and kurta-pajamas for men.

In some regions, women also wear lehengas and ghagras for special occasions.

The use of turbans, particularly in Rajasthan and Punjab, is a distinctive feature.

South India:

South Indian women often wear sarees, with variations in draping styles.

Men typically don dhotis or lungis, though contemporary clothing is also common.

Traditional jewelry, including temple jewelry, is highly ornate and unique to this region.

East India:

Sarees are prevalent among women, with the Bengal cotton saree (tant) being particularly famous.

Men in Bengal often wear kurta-pajamas or dhotis.

Traditional clothing may feature intricate designs, especially during festivals.

West India:

In Gujarat, women favor colorful sarees with intricate bandhani or tie-dye patterns.

Men commonly wear dhoti-kurta or kurtas with churidars.

In Rajasthan, vibrant ghagras (long skirts) and turbans are emblematic.

Traditions:

North India:

The region celebrates festivals like Diwali, Holi, and Karva Chauth with great enthusiasm.

Wedding customs often involve grand processions and elaborate rituals.

South India:

Temples play a central role in daily life and festivities, with rituals and music being unique to this region.

Festivals like Pongal and Onam are celebrated with traditional rituals and feasts.

East India:

The Durga Puja festival in West Bengal is marked by elaborately crafted idols and grand processions.

Odissi and Manipuri dance forms are unique to this region.

West India:

The colorful Navratri celebrations, marked by Garba and Dandiya dance, are famous in Gujarat.

The state of Maharashtra has a vibrant tradition of Ganesh Chaturthi celebrations.

In summary, India's regional diversity in food, clothing, and traditions is a testament to the country's cultural richness. It highlights the unique identities of various regions, each contributing to the vibrant mosaic of Indian culture. These regional variations add depth and complexity to India's cultural heritage, making it a source of fascination and admiration around the world.

# C. The role of festivals in celebrating diversity

Festivals in India are not merely occasions for merrymaking; they are vibrant reflections of the nation's rich tapestry of diversity. These celebrations, steeped in tradition and cultural significance, play a pivotal role in fostering unity, understanding, and the celebration of differences. Here's an exploration of the role of festivals in celebrating diversity in India:

Cultural Showcases:

India's festivals often serve as cultural showcases, spotlighting the diverse traditions, art forms, and cuisines from various regions.

For example, Navratri and Garba in Gujarat, Pongal in Tamil Nadu, and Bihu in Assam celebrate regional harvest traditions with unique rituals and festive foods.

Religious Harmony:

Many Indian festivals have religious origins but are celebrated by people of all faiths.

Diwali, the festival of lights, is celebrated by Hindus, Sikhs, Jains, and some Buddhists, symbolizing the victory of light over darkness and knowledge over ignorance.

Eid ul-Fitr and Eid ul-Adha are celebrated by Muslims, but their warmth extends to neighbors and friends of all backgrounds, reinforcing communal bonds.

Language and Music:

Festivals often incorporate diverse languages, music, and dance forms, showcasing India's linguistic and artistic variety.

The Baisakhi festival in Punjab, for instance, features the energetic Bhangra dance, while Onam in Kerala highlights traditional Kathakali performances.

Secular Celebrations:

Some festivals, like India's Independence Day and Republic Day, are secular celebrations that unite the entire nation.

These occasions emphasize the principles of unity and diversity as citizens from diverse backgrounds come together to commemorate the nation's history.

Fusion and Syncretism:

Festivals in India often witness the fusion of diverse cultural elements.

Christmas in India, for example, incorporates Indian spices and flavors into traditional Christmas dishes, creating a unique blend of Western and Indian culinary traditions.

Social Inclusivity:

Festivals are occasions when people from various socio-economic backgrounds come together to celebrate.

During Holi, the festival of colors, social barriers are temporarily erased as people from all walks of life joyfully participate in the revelry.

Interfaith Understanding:

Festivals provide opportunities for interfaith dialogue and understanding.

The annual Urs festival at Ajmer Sharif, dedicated to the Sufi saint Moinuddin Chishti, welcomes people of all religions to seek spiritual blessings.

National Unity:

National festivals like Republic Day and Independence Day reinforce the idea of a unified India, where diverse cultures and states stand together.

They symbolize the strength that comes from embracing diversity while upholding a common identity.

In summary, festivals in India serve as powerful conduits for celebrating diversity while promoting unity. They are occasions when the nation comes alive with a kaleidoscope of traditions, languages, and beliefs, reminding everyone that India's strength lies in its harmonious coexistence of differences.

# IV. Linguistic Diversity

India, often celebrated as the world's largest democracy, is equally renowned for its extraordinary linguistic diversity. It is a land where language serves as both a bridge and a barrier, where each tongue is a melody that resonates with a unique cultural heritage. Amid this linguistic symphony, the profound concept of "Unity Lies in Diversity" finds one of its most resonant expressions.

In the heart of the Indian subcontinent, a linguistic kaleidoscope unfolds, revealing a tapestry of over 19,000 languages and dialects. While this diversity is nothing short of astounding, it is the unity that emerges from this linguistic mosaic that truly captivates the soul. India's linguistic diversity reflects a paradoxical harmony, a celebration of differences, and a testament to the enduring spirit of coexistence.

In this exploration of linguistic diversity in India, we embark on a journey that traverses the linguistic landscapes of its states, regions, and communities. We delve into the origins, evolution, and preservation of languages that have been nurtured over millennia. From the lyrical cadence of Sanskrit to the rhythmic poetry of Tamil, from the intricate script of Bengali to the tonal melodies of Punjabi, India's linguistic heritage is an unbroken thread that weaves the nation together.

The linguistic diversity of India is a powerful expression of the country's multiculturalism. It mirrors the kaleidoscope of religions, traditions, and customs, offering a lens through which we can glimpse the rich tapestry of Indian society. Beyond mere words, language in

India encapsulates cultural nuances, historical legacies, and the indomitable spirit of a people who have found strength in their differences.

In this context, we will explore the regional variations in language, the literary masterpieces that have shaped India's linguistic identity, and the role of language in everyday life. We will also delve into the challenges of linguistic preservation, revitalization, and the promotion of linguistic diversity in a rapidly evolving world.

As we navigate the linguistic diversity of India, we will uncover stories of resilience, communication, and cultural pride. We will witness the power of language to connect hearts, transcend boundaries, and foster unity. India's linguistic diversity is not a cacophony; it is a symphony, a harmonious blend of voices that together proclaim that "Unity Lies in Diversity." In celebrating this linguistic heritage, we pay homage to the enduring legacy of India, where languages are not just words but the very essence of a nation's identity.

# A. The Multitude of Languages Spoken in India

India, a subcontinent known for its diversity in all aspects of life, boasts an astonishing array of languages that reflect its pluralistic and multicultural character. The multitude of languages spoken in India is nothing short of remarkable, with each language representing a distinct facet of the nation's rich heritage. Here is an overview of this linguistic tapestry:

Official Languages:

The Constitution of India recognizes 22 officially scheduled languages, including Hindi and English at the national level.

Hindi, written in the Devanagari script, is the most widely spoken language in India and serves as a link language among different regions.

English plays a significant role in education, administration, and communication.

Linguistic Diversity:

India is home to over 19,000 languages and dialects, reflecting the country's extraordinary linguistic diversity.

These languages are spread across various states, regions, and communities, creating a unique linguistic mosaic.

The Dravidian Family:

In South India, the Dravidian language family predominates. Tamil, Telugu, Kannada, and Malayalam are some of the major Dravidian languages.

Tamil, with its rich literary tradition dating back over 2,000 years, is one of the oldest languages in the world.

Indo-Aryan Languages:

The Indo-Aryan language family includes languages such as Bengali, Marathi, Gujarati, Punjabi, and Odia.

Each Indo-Aryan language has its own script, culture, and literary tradition.

Other Major Languages:

Assamese, in the Brahmaputra Valley, is the official language of Assam.

Kashmiri is spoken in the northernmost region of Jammu and Kashmir.

Konkani, predominantly spoken in Goa, reflects the state's unique blend of Indian and Portuguese influences.

Manipuri is the official language of Manipur, known for its distinct script and cultural heritage.

Tribal Languages:

India's tribal communities contribute significantly to linguistic diversity. Languages spoken by these communities vary widely from state to state.

Many tribal languages are endangered, emphasizing the importance of language preservation efforts.

Scripts and Writing Systems:

India showcases a rich tapestry of scripts, each intricately linked to its respective language.

Scripts range from the Brahmi-derived scripts like Devanagari (used for Sanskrit and several North Indian languages) to Tamil script, Kannada script, and various regional scripts.

Language Preservation and Promotion:

The Indian government and various linguistic organizations are dedicated to preserving and promoting endangered languages.

Efforts include creating dictionaries, teaching materials, and digital resources to revitalize languages with dwindling speakers.

India's linguistic diversity is a testament to the nation's multicultural heritage, where languages are not merely a means of communication but vessels of culture, history, and identity. In this vast linguistic tapestry, India finds unity amid diversity, celebrating the harmonious coexistence of languages that form an integral part of the country's rich and vibrant mosaic.

# B. Importance of Preserving and Promoting Linguistic Diversity in India

The preservation and promotion of linguistic diversity in India are not just matters of cultural significance but essential pillars of the nation's unity, heritage, and social fabric. Here's an exploration of the profound importance of safeguarding and nurturing India's linguistic diversity:

Cultural Identity:

Language is intrinsically linked to culture. Each language carries with it a unique worldview, traditions, and historical narratives.

Preserving languages means preserving the rich cultural heritage and identities of diverse communities across India.

Inclusivity and Social Cohesion:

Linguistic diversity fosters inclusivity and social cohesion by allowing people to communicate and connect with their roots and communities.

It helps bridge gaps between generations, ensuring that cultural and traditional knowledge is passed down.

Access to Education:

Promoting regional languages in education facilitates better comprehension and engagement among students, especially in the early years of schooling.

It enhances access to education for children from linguistic minorities who may struggle with languages not spoken at home.

Preservation of Indigenous Knowledge:

Many indigenous languages are repositories of ancient knowledge about local ecosystems, medicinal plants, and sustainable practices.

Preserving these languages is crucial for the survival of this invaluable knowledge.

Diverse Perspectives:

Linguistic diversity encourages diverse perspectives and problem-solving approaches, which can be valuable in fields such as science, arts, and governance.

Multilingual societies tend to be more innovative and adaptable.

Economic Benefits:

Multilingualism can be an economic asset. Speaking multiple languages can enhance job prospects and contribute to economic growth.

Preserving languages spoken in tourism-rich regions can boost cultural tourism and local economies.

Preventing Language Extinction:

Many languages in India are endangered, with only a few elderly speakers remaining.

Language preservation efforts are essential to prevent the extinction of these languages, along with the loss of cultural and historical knowledge.

Promoting Social Equity:

Linguistic diversity is integral to social equity. Promoting and preserving languages of marginalized communities empowers them and helps bridge social disparities.

Fostering National Integration:

India's linguistic diversity can be a source of national strength. Recognizing and respecting all languages contribute to a sense of belonging and unity.

It helps counter linguistic chauvinism and promotes the idea that India's unity lies in its diversity.

Global Cultural Contribution:

India's linguistic diversity enriches the global cultural tapestry. Languages like Sanskrit, Hindi, and Tamil have had a profound impact on world literature, philosophy, and science.

In conclusion, the preservation and promotion of linguistic diversity in India are not just about safeguarding languages but nurturing the essence of India itself. These efforts support cultural richness, social cohesion, economic prosperity, and a harmonious national identity. They echo the belief that India's cultural mosaic is incomplete without the vibrant colors of its myriad languages, each telling a unique story of the nation's unity amid its glorious diversity.

# C. The Role of Hindi and English as Link Languages in India

In the diverse linguistic landscape of India, Hindi and English serve as essential link languages, playing pivotal roles in communication, administration, education, and national integration. Here's an exploration of the significance of Hindi and English as link languages in India:

Hindi as a Link Language:

Linguistic Bridge:

Hindi, written in the Devanagari script, acts as a linguistic bridge, connecting people from different regions and linguistic backgrounds.

It serves as a means of communication for Indians whose native languages are different, fostering unity amid linguistic diversity.

Official Language:

Hindi holds the status of an official language at the national level in India, as per the Eighth Schedule of the Constitution.

It is used for official communication between the central government and states that have adopted it as their official language.

Education and Media:

Hindi is a medium of instruction in schools and universities in many states.

It is widely used in print, broadcast, and digital media, making it accessible to a large portion of the population.

Cultural Significance:

Hindi is deeply intertwined with India's cultural heritage and has a rich literary tradition. It is the language of famous poets and authors like Kabir, Tulsidas, and Premchand.

Bollywood, India's prolific film industry, predominantly uses Hindi, making Hindi films a cultural phenomenon across the nation.

Hindi as a Second Language:

In states where Hindi is not the native language, it is often taught as a second language in schools.

This facilitates inter-state and inter-community communication.

English as a Link Language:

Global Communication:

English is recognized worldwide as a global lingua franca, making it indispensable for international communication, trade, and diplomacy.

Proficiency in English opens doors to global opportunities and fosters India's participation in the global economy.

Education and Higher Studies:

English is widely used as a medium of instruction in higher education, especially in fields like science, technology, and business.

It provides access to a vast body of global knowledge and research.

Administration and Governance:

English remains an important language for administration, judiciary, and government communication at the national and state levels.

Legal documents, official reports, and government notifications are often published in English.

Business and Industry:

English proficiency is an asset in India's growing business and IT sectors, attracting foreign investment and global companies.

It facilitates cross-cultural collaboration and trade.

Access to Information:

English is the language of the internet, science, and technology, enabling Indians to access information, research, and innovation from around the world.

National Integration:

English helps bridge linguistic gaps within India by providing a common language for communication among people from diverse linguistic backgrounds.

While Hindi and English play crucial roles as link languages, it's essential to recognize that linguistic diversity remains a cherished aspect of India's identity. Language policies should balance the promotion of these languages with the preservation and support of regional languages and dialects, ensuring that India continues to celebrate its unity amid diversity.

# V. Religious Diversity

India, a land where spirituality and faith have woven a tapestry as intricate as it is diverse, stands as a beacon of religious pluralism. In the vibrant mosaic of this ancient nation, the profound concept that "Unity Lies in Diversity" finds its most profound expression through its religious richness. India's religious diversity is a testament to the coexistence of myriad faiths, beliefs, and practices, reflecting a profound respect for the sacred, the spiritual, and the divine.

Nestled within the embrace of India's geographical contours, a kaleidoscope of religions and belief systems flourish. From the sacred banks of the Ganges, where Hinduism finds its epicenter, to the birthplace of Buddhism under the Bodhi Tree, to the tranquil serenity of Sikhism's Golden Temple, and the vibrant mosaic of mosques, churches, synagogues, and gurdwaras, India's religious landscape is an epic narrative of faith, devotion, and interfaith dialogue.

In this exploration of religious diversity in India, we embark on a journey that traverses the spiritual landscapes of its regions, states, and communities. We delve into the origins, evolution, and sacred practices of major religions, from the ancient philosophies of Hinduism, Buddhism, Jainism, and Sikhism to the Abrahamic faiths of Islam, Christianity, Judaism, and Zoroastrianism.

India's religious diversity extends far beyond faith alone. It is deeply rooted in the nation's social fabric, cultural heritage, and even its political identity. Over millennia, India has embraced an ethos of tolerance, respect, and acceptance, where diverse religious communities have not only found sanctuary but also the freedom to flourish and enrich the nation's tapestry of spirituality.

In this context, we will explore the coexistence of sacred sites, the rituals and festivals that unite people of various faiths, and the role of spiritual leaders and saints who have transcended religious boundaries to spread messages of peace and universal brotherhood.

Religious diversity in India is not without its challenges and complexities, from historical conflicts to contemporary issues. Yet, it is precisely in these complexities that the nation's commitment to unity shines most brightly. Through dialogue, interfaith initiatives, and constitutional safeguards, India continues to navigate the delicate balance between the plurality of beliefs and the unity of its people.

Ultimately, India's religious diversity is a source of strength, an embodiment of the enduring idea that, in this land of myriad gods and diverse paths, unity thrives. It is a testament to the coexistence of spiritual aspirations and communal cohesion, reminding the world that the pursuit of the divine can walk hand in hand with the celebration of differences. In exploring India's religious diversity, we seek not only to understand but also to celebrate the remarkable tapestry of faiths that together proclaim that "Unity Lies in Diversity."

# A. Major Religions in India - A Tapestry of Faith and Belief

India is a land where spirituality flows through the veins of its people, and religious diversity is woven into the very fabric of its society. The nation is home to a rich tapestry of major religions, each with its unique beliefs, practices, and profound historical significance. Here is an overview of the major religions that flourish in India:

1. Hinduism:

Hinduism, often referred to as the world's oldest religion, has deep roots in India. It encompasses a wide range of beliefs, rituals, and philosophies.

Core tenets include karma (the law of cause and effect), dharma (duty and righteousness), and moksha (liberation from the cycle of reincarnation).

Hinduism boasts a pantheon of deities, with gods like Brahma, Vishnu, and Shiva, and a multitude of scriptures, including the Vedas, Upanishads, and Bhagavad Gita.

2. Islam:

Islam, introduced to India in the 7th century, is one of the country's major religions.

Followers, known as Muslims, adhere to the teachings of the Quran and follow the Five Pillars of Islam, including prayer, fasting, and charity.

India has a significant Muslim population, with historical monuments like the Taj Mahal and Qutb Minar showcasing Islamic architecture.

3. Christianity:

Christianity arrived in India around the 1st century, and India has a diverse Christian community.

The faith is centered on the teachings of Jesus Christ and the Bible.

India's Christian community includes Catholics, Protestants, and Eastern Orthodox believers, each with distinct practices and traditions.

4. Sikhism:

Sikhism, founded in the Punjab region in the 15th century by Guru Nanak Dev Ji, emphasizes monotheism and equality.

The Golden Temple in Amritsar is one of Sikhism's holiest sites.

Sikhs follow the Guru Granth Sahib, their holy scripture, and live by principles such as community service and selflessness.

5. Buddhism:

Buddhism, born in India in the 6th century BCE through the teachings of Siddhartha Gautama (Buddha), emphasizes the Four Noble Truths and the Eightfold Path.

India is home to important Buddhist sites like Bodh Gaya, where Buddha attained enlightenment, and Sarnath, where he gave his first sermon.

6. Jainism:

Jainism, founded in India in the 6th century BCE, emphasizes non-violence (ahimsa), truthfulness, and self-discipline.

Jain monks and nuns practice extreme asceticism, striving for spiritual purity.

Prominent Jain pilgrimage sites include Palitana and Shravanabelagola.

7. Zoroastrianism:

India is home to a small but ancient Zoroastrian community known as Parsis.

Zoroastrianism, founded by the prophet Zoroaster (Zarathustra), emphasizes the dualism of good and evil and the worship of Ahura Mazda.

8. Indigenous and Tribal Religions:

India's indigenous communities practice diverse tribal religions, often closely connected to nature and local deities.

These traditions are rich in rituals, storytelling, and oral traditions.

9. Other Religions:

India is also home to smaller communities of Jews, Bahá'ís, Sikhs, and followers of newer spiritual movements.

This tapestry of religions in India is a testament to the nation's profound respect for spirituality and the freedom of religious expression. It reflects the ethos that "Unity Lies in Diversity," as Indians of various faiths coexist harmoniously, celebrating their shared values while cherishing the unique beauty of their individual beliefs and traditions.

# B. Interactions and Coexistence of Various Religious Communities in India

India's long history is marked by a tapestry of interactions and coexistence among various religious communities. This coexistence, often referred to as "unity in diversity," is a hallmark of the nation's rich cultural and social fabric. Here's an exploration of how different religious communities in India have interacted and coexisted over the centuries:

1. Interfaith Dialogue:

India has a long tradition of interfaith dialogue, where scholars, sages, and religious leaders from diverse backgrounds have engaged in discussions, debates, and exchanges of ideas.

These dialogues have enriched religious thought, fostered understanding, and contributed to the harmonious coexistence of faiths.

2. Shared Festivals:

India's diverse religious communities often celebrate each other's festivals with enthusiasm and respect.

Diwali, the Hindu festival of lights, is celebrated by people of various faiths, while Christmas and Eid are observed by many non-Christian and non-Muslim communities, respectively.

3. Places of Worship:

India is home to places of worship from various religions in close proximity to one another.

Cities like Varanasi showcase the peaceful coexistence of Hindu temples, mosques, and Buddhist stupas along the Ganges River.

4. Syncretic Traditions:

Some regions of India have nurtured syncretic traditions that blend elements of different faiths.

For example, Sufi saints like Moinuddin Chishti in Ajmer have drawn devotees from Hindu and Muslim communities alike.

5. Spiritual Leaders and Reformers:

Spiritual leaders and reformers like Swami Vivekananda, who represented Hinduism at the Parliament of the World's Religions in 1893, emphasized the universality of spiritual principles.

Leaders like Mahatma Gandhi promoted religious tolerance and unity in the struggle for independence.

6. Constitutional Safeguards:

India's Constitution guarantees freedom of religion and the right to practice, profess, and propagate one's faith.

It also recognizes the importance of preserving and promoting the diverse cultures and religions of India.

7. Communal Harmony Movements:

Various social and religious organizations in India actively work to promote communal harmony and bridge religious divides.

Initiatives such as interfaith peace dialogues, cultural exchanges, and community service projects aim to foster understanding and tolerance.

8. Joint Celebrations and Pilgrimages:

In some regions, people of different faiths organize joint celebrations and pilgrimages to promote unity and solidarity.

This is particularly evident in regions with shared religious heritage and legends.

9. Legal Framework for Dispute Resolution:

India has a legal framework for resolving disputes related to religious sites, often involving multiple faiths.

These mechanisms aim to ensure that conflicts are resolved peacefully and with respect for all communities involved.

While India's history is replete with examples of religious harmony and coexistence, it is important to acknowledge that challenges and tensions have also existed at various times. However, the enduring spirit of unity amid diversity remains a defining feature of India's social and cultural landscape. The nation continues to work toward fostering greater understanding, tolerance, and cooperation among its diverse religious communities, exemplifying the belief that religious diversity is a source of strength and enrichment for all.

# C. Religious Tolerance and Secularism in the Indian Constitution

India's Constitution, adopted on January 26, 1950, reflects a commitment to religious tolerance and secularism, principles that are enshrined in its foundational document. These principles serve as the bedrock of India's diverse and pluralistic society. Here's an exploration of how religious tolerance and secularism are embedded in the Indian Constitution:

1. Preamble:

The Preamble of the Indian Constitution declares India to be a "sovereign, socialist, secular, and democratic republic."

The term "secular" was added during the 42nd Amendment Act in 1976, emphasizing the secular nature of the Indian state.

2. Fundamental Rights:

Part III of the Constitution guarantees fundamental rights to all citizens, regardless of their religion. These rights include the freedom of religion and the right to equality.

Article 25 ensures the freedom of conscience and the right to freely profess, practice, and propagate religion.

Article 26 protects the right of religious denominations and institutions to manage their affairs.

3. Equality Before Law:

Article 15 prohibits discrimination on the grounds of religion, race, caste, sex, or place of birth.

This ensures that no citizen is denied access to public places, goods, services, or employment opportunities based on their religious beliefs.

4. Religious Freedom and Conversion:

While Article 25 guarantees the freedom to propagate religion, it also allows the state to regulate religious practices.

Some states have enacted laws regulating religious conversion to prevent coercion or fraudulent inducement.

5. Personal Laws:

The Indian Constitution respects personal laws based on religion. It allows individuals to be governed by their respective personal laws in matters of marriage, divorce, and succession.

However, the state has the authority to reform personal laws to ensure gender equality and social justice, as demonstrated by the reforms in Muslim personal law, such as the outlawing of triple talaq.

6. Secular State:

India is a secular state, which means that the government does not promote or favor any particular religion.

The state remains neutral in religious matters and does not interfere in religious practices, rituals, or beliefs.

7. Equal Treatment of Religions:

The Indian state treats all religions and religious groups equally.

It provides financial support to religious minorities to protect and preserve their cultural and educational institutions.

8. Freedom of Religious Instruction:

Article 28 prohibits religious instruction in educational institutions wholly maintained by the state.

However, religious instruction may be provided in institutions not wholly maintained by the state, with the consent of guardians.

9. Protection of Places of Worship:

The Constitution acknowledges the importance of protecting places of worship and their sanctity.

It seeks to prevent desecration or harm to religious sites.

10. Amending Religious Provisions:

- Certain provisions related to religious matters can be amended by a two-thirds majority in Parliament.

- However, the "basic structure" of the Constitution, which includes its secular character, cannot be altered.

These constitutional provisions reflect India's commitment to religious tolerance and secularism. They aim to ensure that all citizens can practice their faith freely while safeguarding the principle that the state does not favor any particular religion. Despite the complexities of managing a diverse religious landscape, India's secular and pluralistic principles continue to be an integral part of the nation's identity, fostering unity amid its rich tapestry of faiths and beliefs.

# VI. Social and Ethnic Diversity

India, often celebrated as the world's largest democracy, is equally renowned for its remarkable social and ethnic diversity. It is a nation where every step unveils a new facet of human existence, where traditions, cultures, languages, and lifestyles converge in a tapestry that is as intricate as it is vibrant. Within this diverse panorama, the profound concept of "Unity Lies in Diversity" finds its most profound expression.

Nestled within the geographical expanse of the Indian subcontinent is a living kaleidoscope of ethnicities, communities, and social groups. From the snow-clad peaks of the Himalayas to the sun-soaked shores of the Indian Ocean, India's social and ethnic diversity forms the essence of its identity. It is the harmonious blend of these varied identities that transcends mere existence and creates a sense of belonging and unity.

In this exploration of social and ethnic diversity in India, we embark on a journey that traverses the landscapes of its states, regions, and communities. We delve into the origins, traditions, and narratives that define the mosaic of ethnicities, from the indigenous tribes of the Northeast to the vibrant communities of the South, and from the rich tapestry of North India to the dynamic cultural exchanges of the West.

India's social and ethnic diversity extends beyond mere demographics; it is a profound tapestry of traditions, practices, languages, and identities. It mirrors the kaleidoscope of religious beliefs, culinary delights, artistic expressions, and political landscapes, offering a lens through which we can glimpse the rich tapestry of Indian society.

In this context, we will explore the dynamic interactions between social groups, the shared festivals that transcend ethnic boundaries, and the role of cultural icons who have become bridges of understanding and respect. We will also delve into the challenges and triumphs of India's ongoing journey toward social harmony, inclusivity, and equitable development.

Social and ethnic diversity in India is not without its complexities, historical legacies, and contemporary challenges. Yet, it is precisely in these complexities that India's spirit of unity and resilience shines most brightly. Through dialogue, cultural exchanges, and constitutional safeguards, India continues to navigate the intricate interplay of its diverse communities, exemplifying the belief that "Unity Lies in Diversity."

In celebrating this social and ethnic diversity, we acknowledge that it is not just the sum of its parts but the very essence of India itself. It is a reminder that while people may come from different backgrounds, cultures, and histories, they share the common ground of being a part of the incredible mosaic that is India, where unity thrives amid its magnificent diversity.

### A. Caste System and Its Impact on Social Diversity in India

The caste system is a deeply ingrained social hierarchy that has significantly influenced the social diversity of India for centuries. It is a complex system of social stratification based on birth, with individuals categorized into distinct groups known as castes or jatis. The caste system has left a profound impact on Indian society, affecting various aspects of life, including social interactions, access to resources, and economic opportunities. Here's an exploration of the caste system's impact on social diversity in India:

1. Historical Origins:

The origins of the caste system are ancient and complex, with historical roots dating back thousands of years.

It is believed to have evolved from the Varna system mentioned in ancient scriptures, which classified society into four main varnas or classes: Brahmins (priests and scholars), Kshatriyas (warriors and rulers), Vaishyas (merchants and farmers), and Shudras (laborers and servants).

Over time, this system expanded to include numerous castes and sub-castes.

2. Social Hierarchies:

The caste system classifies individuals into rigid social hierarchies, with each caste having its own status, occupation, and social privileges.

Brahmins are traditionally considered the highest caste, followed by Kshatriyas, Vaishyas, and Shudras. Below the Shudras are the Dalits (formerly known as untouchables), who historically faced severe discrimination and exclusion.

3. Occupational Roles:

Castes often dictate the occupations individuals are expected to pursue. This occupational stratification has limited social mobility and economic opportunities for those born into lower castes.

The stigma associated with certain occupations has contributed to the perpetuation of caste-based discrimination.

4. Social Segregation:

The caste system has historically led to social segregation, with individuals from different castes living in separate neighborhoods, attending separate schools, and even drinking water from separate sources.

Inter-caste marriages were, and in some regions still are, heavily discouraged or met with resistance.

5. Discrimination and Untouchability:

The caste system has perpetuated discrimination and the practice of untouchability against Dalits, who were considered impure and subjected to severe social exclusion.

The Indian Constitution has outlawed untouchability and provides affirmative action measures to uplift Dalits, known as Scheduled Castes, and other marginalized communities.

6. Political Representation:

The caste system has had a profound impact on Indian politics, with political parties often seeking to align themselves with particular caste groups to gain electoral support.

Reservation policies provide reserved seats in educational institutions and government jobs for Scheduled Castes, Scheduled Tribes, and Other Backward Classes (OBCs) to address historical injustices.

7. Ongoing Challenges:

Despite legal reforms and efforts to promote social equality, the caste system continues to influence social dynamics in India.

Discrimination, violence, and social ostracism against lower-caste individuals and Dalits persist in various parts of the country.

While efforts to eradicate caste-based discrimination and promote social diversity are ongoing, the caste system's deep-rooted impact remains a complex and evolving challenge for India. It reflects the ongoing struggle to balance the preservation of cultural diversity with the pursuit of social equality and justice, highlighting the enduring significance of addressing social diversity within the nation.

# B. Tribal Communities and Their Unique Cultural Practices in India

India's social diversity extends to its numerous tribal communities, often referred to as Adivasis or Scheduled Tribes. These indigenous groups are an integral part of the country's rich cultural tapestry and contribute to the nation's ethos of unity in diversity. Tribal communities in India are known for their distinctive cultural practices, which reflect their deep connection to nature, spirituality, and traditions. Here's an exploration of tribal communities and their unique cultural practices:

1. Diverse Tribal Population:

India is home to over 700 distinct tribal groups, each with its own language, customs, and way of life.

These communities are spread across various states and regions, with a significant presence in states like Jharkhand, Chhattisgarh, Odisha, and the northeastern states.

2. Connection to Nature:

Tribal communities maintain a close relationship with nature and often inhabit forested and hilly regions.

Their traditional lifestyles are intertwined with agriculture, hunting, gathering, and sustainable practices that preserve the environment.

3. Unique Languages and Dialects:

Tribal communities often have their own languages or dialects, preserving ancient linguistic traditions.

These languages are an essential part of their identity and cultural heritage.

4. Rituals and Festivals:

Tribal festivals and rituals are colorful and vibrant, reflecting their deep spirituality and reverence for nature.

Festivals like Bihu in Assam, Jatra in Jharkhand, and Bastar Dussehra in Chhattisgarh celebrate the changing seasons and important milestones in their lives.

5. Traditional Art and Crafts:

Tribal communities are known for their intricate art forms and craftsmanship, including pottery, basket weaving, wood carving, and tribal jewelry.

These traditional skills are passed down through generations.

6. Music and Dance:

Tribal music and dance are integral to their cultural expression.

Instruments like drums, flutes, and gongs are used in rhythmic performances that celebrate life, harvest, and various rituals.

7. Oral Traditions:

Tribal communities have a rich oral tradition, with stories, myths, and folklore passed down through generations.

These stories often revolve around their relationship with the natural world and their ancestors.

8. Social Structures:

Many tribal communities have egalitarian social structures, where decision-making is collective and leadership is often based on age and experience.

Traditional councils or village assemblies play a significant role in resolving disputes and making community decisions.

9. Challenges and Preservation:

Tribal communities in India face various challenges, including land displacement, lack of access to education and healthcare, and economic marginalization.

Efforts are being made to preserve their unique cultural practices and protect their rights through constitutional safeguards and affirmative action measures.

Tribal communities in India are not frozen in time; they adapt and evolve while preserving their core cultural values. Their unique traditions and practices enrich the nation's cultural diversity, reminding us that unity can coexist with diversity. Recognizing and respecting the rich cultural heritage of tribal communities is not only a matter of social justice but also an opportunity to learn from their sustainable and harmonious relationship with the natural world.

# C. Efforts to Promote Social Inclusivity and Equality in India

India's journey toward social inclusivity and equality has been marked by both progress and challenges. The nation has made concerted efforts to bridge the gaps of inequality, uplift marginalized communities, and promote social cohesion. Here are key efforts and initiatives aimed at fostering social inclusivity and equality in India:

1. Reservation Policies:

The Indian Constitution provides for affirmative action through reservation policies. Scheduled Castes (SCs), Scheduled Tribes (STs), and Other Backward Classes (OBCs) are given reserved seats in educational institutions, government jobs, and legislative bodies.

These policies aim to address historical discrimination and underrepresentation.

2. Social Welfare Programs:

Various social welfare programs, such as the National Rural Employment Guarantee Act (MGNREGA) and the Integrated Child Development Services (ICDS) scheme, target vulnerable populations.

These programs provide employment opportunities, nutrition, and healthcare services to marginalized communities.

3. Land Reforms:

Land reform initiatives seek to redistribute land to landless agricultural laborers and marginalized communities.

Land ownership and access to land are critical for economic empowerment and social inclusion.

4. Reservation for Women:

In local governance institutions (Panchayats and Municipalities), a significant proportion of seats are reserved for women.

This promotes women's participation in decision-making and governance.

5. Legal Measures:

The legal framework includes laws against discrimination, such as the Scheduled Castes and Scheduled Tribes (Prevention of Atrocities) Act and anti-discrimination provisions in labor laws.

These laws protect the rights and dignity of marginalized communities.

6. Education and Scholarships:

Scholarships and financial incentives are provided to students from marginalized communities to promote access to quality education.

Schemes like the Post-Matric Scholarship for SC/ST students support higher education.

7. Awareness and Sensitization:

Efforts are made to raise awareness and sensitize society to issues of discrimination and inequality.

Educational campaigns, media initiatives, and community engagement programs play a crucial role.

8. Social Movements and Civil Society:

Grassroots movements and civil society organizations actively work to promote social inclusivity and advocate for the rights of marginalized communities.

They provide support, representation, and a platform for marginalized voices.

9. Economic Development Programs:

Economic development programs, like the National Rural Livelihoods Mission (NRLM), focus on livelihood enhancement and economic empowerment of marginalized communities.

These programs encourage entrepreneurship and self-sufficiency.

10. Access to Healthcare:

- Initiatives like the National Health Mission (NHM) aim to improve healthcare access and services in underserved areas, benefiting marginalized populations.

11. Constitutional Safeguards:

- The Indian Constitution includes provisions that guarantee the protection and promotion of the rights of SCs, STs, and other marginalized communities.

- These safeguards are crucial for ensuring social inclusivity and equality.

While these efforts demonstrate India's commitment to social inclusivity and equality, challenges persist. Issues like caste-based discrimination, unequal access to resources, and economic disparities require sustained efforts and comprehensive strategies. Nevertheless, India's progress in promoting social inclusivity and equality is a testament to its commitment to realizing the vision of "Unity Lies in Diversity" by ensuring that every citizen has the opportunity to participate fully in the nation's social and economic life.

# VII. Political Unity

India, a land known for its breathtaking geographical diversity, ancient cultural heritage, and a tapestry of languages and traditions, also stands as a remarkable testament to the enduring concept that "Unity Lies in Diversity." Amidst this mosaic of identities and backgrounds, one of India's most remarkable achievements is its political unity—a unity that binds together over a billion people, representing a kaleidoscope of beliefs, languages, and cultures.

The story of India's political unity is one of profound significance, where the democratic spirit triumphs over differences, forging a collective identity that transcends the boundaries of region, religion, and ethnicity. In a nation where hundreds of languages are spoken, diverse cuisines savored, and countless gods worshipped, the principles of democracy, pluralism, and federalism serve as the pillars upon which this political unity is built.

In this exploration of political unity in India, we embark on a journey that unveils the intricacies of a vast and complex democracy. We delve into the historical milestones, the democratic institutions, and the principles that have guided India's political landscape since gaining independence from colonial rule in 1947.

India's political unity extends from the federal structure of governance, where the nation is a union of states and union territories, each with its own unique character and governance. We examine the role of the Indian Parliament, a dynamic forum where diverse voices from across the nation come together to shape laws and policies that reflect the aspirations of a vast and varied population.

The electoral process, often dubbed the "festival of democracy," is a testament to India's commitment to political unity. Millions of citizens exercise their right to vote in a process that spans weeks and multiple phases, ensuring that the diversity of opinions and perspectives finds expression in the nation's leadership.

This exploration also considers the challenges and complexities that India faces in maintaining political unity. Issues such as regional aspirations, linguistic diversity, and the balance between state autonomy and central authority continue to shape the nation's political discourse.

In celebrating India's political unity, we acknowledge that it is not just the coexistence of different states and regions but the very essence of the nation itself. It is a reminder that despite its diversity, India stands as one, bound by the principles of democracy and the collective aspiration for a better future. It is a living testament to the enduring belief that "Unity Lies in Diversity," where the richness of cultures and traditions only serves to strengthen the nation's democratic fabric and propel it forward on the path of progress and social justice.

# A. India's Struggle for Independence and the Role of Unity in Diversity

India's struggle for independence from British colonial rule was a momentous chapter in its history, and it exemplified the profound principle that "Unity Lies in Diversity." The movement for freedom was marked by the coming together of people from diverse backgrounds, cultures, and ideologies under the common goal of liberation. Here's an exploration of India's struggle for independence and the pivotal role played by unity in diversity:

1. Diverse Leadership:

India's independence movement was led by a diverse group of leaders representing various religious, linguistic, and cultural backgrounds.

Prominent leaders like Mahatma Gandhi, Jawaharlal Nehru, Sardar Vallabhbhai Patel, and Dr. B.R. Ambedkar represented different regions, religions, and ideologies.

2. Inclusivity and Mass Mobilization:

The struggle for independence was marked by mass mobilization, with people from all walks of life joining the movement.

Freedom fighters came from urban and rural areas, different castes and communities, and various professions.

3. Non-Violence and Unity:

Mahatma Gandhi's philosophy of non-violence (Satyagraha) played a unifying role in the independence movement.

Non-violent protests, boycotts, and civil disobedience campaigns attracted a broad spectrum of Indian society, promoting unity.

4. Interfaith Harmony:

The freedom struggle emphasized interfaith harmony and cooperation.

Leaders from different religions worked together, and religious symbols, such as the spinning wheel (charkha), became powerful symbols of resistance.

5. Linguistic and Cultural Diversity:

India's linguistic and cultural diversity was celebrated in the struggle for independence.

Songs, poems, and literature in various languages played a significant role in inspiring the masses.

6. Regional Solidarity:

Regional leaders and movements, such as the Quit India Movement and the Tebhaga Movement, contributed to the overall effort for independence.

The diverse regional aspirations were accommodated within the broader framework of a united India.

7. Negotiating Unity:

The diversity within India was also addressed during negotiations with the British.

Leaders like Sardar Patel played a crucial role in integrating princely states into the newly independent nation, forging political unity.

8. The Role of Inclusive Symbols:

National symbols like the Indian flag, with its colors representing different communities, and the national anthem, which draws from multiple languages, symbolized India's diversity within unity.

9. Legacy of Inclusivity:

The inclusivity and unity forged during the struggle for independence laid the foundation for the democratic and pluralistic India that emerged in 1947.

India's Constitution, adopted in 1950, enshrines the principles of equality, secularism, and democracy.

10. Ongoing Commitment:

- India's commitment to unity in diversity remains an ongoing effort in the post-independence era.

- The nation continues to address issues related to caste, religion, language, and regional disparities through legal, social, and political means.

India's journey to independence demonstrated that diversity can be a source of strength rather than division. The unity forged during this pivotal period in history serves as a testament to the enduring idea that the nation's strength lies in its ability to celebrate differences, accommodate diverse voices, and work collectively towards a common goal. India's struggle for independence and its subsequent nation-building process exemplify the belief that true unity is achieved when diversity is embraced and respected.

# B. Formation of the Indian Union and Its Diverse States

The formation of the Indian Union in 1947 marked a historic moment in the annals of global politics. As India emerged from the shackles of colonial rule, it faced the monumental task of integrating a vast subcontinent, characterized by its incredible diversity, into a unified nation. This endeavor was not only a political challenge but also a testament to the belief that "Unity Lies in Diversity." Here's an exploration of the formation of the Indian Union and the diverse states that make up this remarkable nation:

1. Partition and Independence:

In 1947, British India was partitioned into two independent nations: India and Pakistan. India gained independence from British colonial rule on August 15, 1947.

2. Integration of Princely States:

One of the most complex tasks facing the newly independent India was the integration of over 500 princely states into the union.

Sardar Vallabhbhai Patel, India's first Deputy Prime Minister and Minister of Home Affairs, played a pivotal role in this process, using diplomacy and negotiation to bring these diverse states into the fold.

3. Linguistic and Cultural Diversity:

India's states are characterized by immense linguistic, cultural, and regional diversity. Each state has its own distinct language, customs, and traditions.

Language has played a significant role in the formation of states and the preservation of cultural identities.

4. Federal Structure:

India adopted a federal system of governance, with a division of powers between the central government and the states.

The Indian Constitution outlines the powers and responsibilities of both levels of government.

5. State Reorganization:

In 1956, India underwent a major reorganization of states on linguistic lines. This led to the creation of states based on the primary language spoken in each region.

The reorganization aimed to accommodate linguistic diversity and foster a sense of cultural identity.

6. State Capitals:

Each state in India has its own capital, often chosen for historical, administrative, or geographical reasons.

Capitals like Mumbai (Maharashtra), Chennai (Tamil Nadu), and Kolkata (West Bengal) are prominent centers of culture, commerce, and governance.

7. Special Provisions:

Some states, such as Jammu and Kashmir, have special provisions under Article 370 of the Indian Constitution.

These provisions grant states varying degrees of autonomy in certain matters.

8. Regional Aspirations:

India's states often have distinct political, economic, and developmental aspirations.

The federal structure accommodates these regional variations and allows for diverse policies and priorities.

9. Unity in Pluralism:

India's diverse states and union territories form a unified political entity that celebrates its pluralism and diversity.

The Indian Union is a testament to the nation's commitment to accommodating differences and fostering unity.

10. Ongoing Challenges and Cooperation:

- While India's states have diverse needs and challenges, they also cooperate in areas such as trade, security, and cultural exchange.

- Organizations like the National Institution for Transforming India (NITI Aayog) facilitate cooperation between the center and the states.

The formation of the Indian Union and the subsequent coexistence of diverse states exemplify the nation's ability to celebrate its differences while working collectively for the common good. This political unity, rooted in diversity, is a testament to the enduring belief that India's strength lies in its ability to accommodate the myriad voices, cultures, and aspirations that make up this incredible nation.

# C. Challenges in Maintaining Political Unity in India

While India's political unity is a remarkable achievement given its diversity, it is not without its challenges. Maintaining political unity in a nation characterized by linguistic, cultural, regional, and religious diversity is an ongoing endeavor. Here are some of the key challenges:

1. Linguistic Diversity:

India is home to hundreds of languages, and linguistic diversity can sometimes lead to linguistic tensions.

States often demand official language status for their regional languages, which can create conflicts and demands for separate states.

2. Regional Aspirations:

Different states within India often have distinct political and economic aspirations.

Regional parties can push for greater autonomy or demand specific policies that may not align with the central government's priorities.

3. Communal Tensions:

Religious diversity can lead to communal tensions, with occasional outbreaks of violence between religious communities.

Maintaining religious harmony and preventing communal conflicts is a constant challenge.

4. Economic Disparities:

Economic disparities exist between different states and regions, leading to variations in development levels.

Bridging these disparities and ensuring equitable economic growth remains a challenge.

5. Resource Allocation:

Disputes over the allocation of resources, particularly water and minerals, can arise between states.

Resolving these disputes while ensuring fair resource sharing is a complex task.

6. Center-State Relations:

Balancing the powers of the central government and the states can be contentious.

States often seek more autonomy and financial resources, leading to debates over the distribution of powers.

7. Ethnic and Tribal Issues:

Ethnic and tribal communities may have unique cultural and developmental needs that require special attention.

Balancing their interests with those of the mainstream population can be challenging.

8. Political Fragmentation:

The proliferation of regional and local parties can lead to fragmented politics, making it difficult to form stable governments at the national level.

9. Security Concerns:

India faces security challenges along its borders, which can strain national unity.

Managing border disputes and addressing security threats is essential for maintaining political unity.

10. Historical Conflicts:

- Some regions have historical conflicts and grievances that persist, affecting political stability.

- These conflicts may require long-term reconciliation efforts.

11. Migration and Demographics:

- Migration within India can alter the demographic makeup of regions and states.

- This can lead to social and political tensions if not managed effectively.

12. Environmental and Climate Challenges:

- Environmental issues, such as water scarcity and climate change, can exacerbate tensions between states, especially in regions dependent on common water sources.

India's ability to address these challenges and maintain political unity is a testament to its commitment to democracy, federalism, and pluralism. The nation's success in navigating its diversity while upholding the principles of unity reflects the enduring belief that diversity is a source of strength and enrichment, and that the unity of India is built upon a foundation that celebrates differences and fosters cooperation.

# VIII. Economic Diversity

India, a nation celebrated for its cultural mosaic, linguistic tapestry, and political unity, also stands as a testament to the profound principle that "Unity Lies in Diversity" in the realm of economics. The Indian subcontinent is a land of stark economic contrasts, where the rhythms of rural agriculture harmonize with the hum of bustling urban centers, and where disparities in wealth and income coexist with the aspirations of a nation striving for economic equity.

The story of India's economic diversity is a testament to the nation's ability to weave together myriad economic narratives into a vibrant tapestry of progress. It is a story of resilience and transformation, where traditional practices meld with modern innovations, and where the economic landscape accommodates the aspirations of a billion-plus citizens.

In this exploration of economic diversity in India, we embark on a journey that traverses the varied terrains of agrarian heartlands, burgeoning industrial hubs, and the dynamic services sector. We delve into the historical underpinnings, contemporary economic landscapes, and the entrepreneurial spirit that underpin India's economic diversity.

India's economic diversity is marked by a rich tapestry of livelihoods, from subsistence farming in rural villages to the technological innovation hubs of urban centers. We examine the role of agriculture, manufacturing, and the services sector in shaping the nation's economic narrative.

The nation's entrepreneurial spirit is celebrated as we explore the emergence of Indian business magnates who have transformed India's economy on the global stage. From traditional artisans to tech pioneers, India's economic diversity reflects a society where innovation, ambition, and hard work are revered.

Challenges, too, are an integral part of India's economic story. Income inequality, regional disparities, and the informal economy pose complex challenges that require innovative policy solutions and inclusive development strategies. We delve into these challenges and the efforts made to address them.

Economic diversity in India is not just about disparities but also about the interplay of cultures, traditions, and aspirations that shape the economic landscape. We celebrate the festivals that mark agricultural seasons, the cultural diversity that enriches trade, and the spirit of entrepreneurship that drives innovation.

In examining India's economic diversity, we recognize that it is not merely an aggregation of income statistics but a vibrant expression of the nation's identity. It is a reminder that while economic disparities exist, the nation's unity thrives amid its diverse economic narratives. The belief that "Unity Lies in Diversity" is exemplified in India's ability to harness its economic diversity as a source of strength, innovation, and resilience, working collectively towards a future that is economically inclusive and equitable for all.

# A. Regional Variations in Economic Development in India

India's economic landscape is marked by significant regional variations in development, reflecting the nation's diverse geography, historical legacies, and varying levels of industrialization. These regional disparities have been a subject of concern and policy attention, as they highlight the complex challenges of balancing economic growth and inclusive development in a vast and diverse nation. Here's an exploration of regional variations in economic development in India:

1. Northern Plains:

The fertile Gangetic plains of northern India have historically been agriculturally prosperous.

States like Punjab and Haryana are known as the "Granaries of India" due to their high agricultural productivity, particularly in wheat and rice.

2. Southern States:

Southern states such as Tamil Nadu, Karnataka, and Kerala have seen significant industrialization and economic diversification.

They have robust manufacturing and services sectors, contributing to their relatively high per capita income.

3. Western States:

Western states like Maharashtra and Gujarat have emerged as economic powerhouses, hosting major industrial and financial hubs.

Mumbai, in Maharashtra, is the financial capital of India, while Gujarat has a strong industrial base.

4. Eastern States:

Eastern states like Bihar, Jharkhand, and Odisha face economic challenges, including lower levels of industrialization and infrastructure development.

Agriculture remains a dominant sector in these regions, with efforts underway to promote industrial growth.

5. Northeastern States:

The northeastern states are characterized by their hilly terrain, which poses logistical challenges.

These states have diverse economies, including agriculture, handicrafts, and tourism, but face infrastructure deficits.

6. Central India:

Central Indian states like Madhya Pradesh and Chhattisgarh have a mix of agriculture and industry.

The region is known for mineral resources and is an important contributor to India's industrial output.

7. Coastal States:

Coastal states like Goa and Kerala benefit from their strategic location and strong tourism sectors.

They have vibrant economies driven by tourism, trade, and services.

8. Union Territories:

Union territories like Delhi and Puducherry have unique economic profiles.

Delhi serves as the national capital and has a diverse economy, while Puducherry relies on tourism and agriculture.

9. Himalayan States:

States in the Himalayan region, such as Himachal Pradesh and Uttarakhand, face geographic constraints but have tapped into tourism and horticulture for economic growth.

10. Urban-Rural Divide:

- Regional disparities often manifest as an urban-rural divide, with urban areas experiencing higher economic growth rates and better access to services.

11. Policy Interventions:

- The Indian government has implemented various policies and programs to address regional disparities, including special economic zones, infrastructure development initiatives, and targeted subsidies.

12. Inclusive Development Goals:

- Efforts are underway to promote inclusive and sustainable development, ensuring that the benefits of economic growth reach marginalized and disadvantaged communities in all regions.

Understanding and addressing regional disparities is a key challenge for India's policymakers. While progress has been made in narrowing these disparities, the nation continues to strive for balanced economic development that ensures every region benefits from the economic growth story. Balancing the diverse needs and potential of India's regions is an ongoing endeavor as the nation works to realize the vision that "Unity Lies in Diversity" not only culturally and politically but also economically.

## B. Contribution of Different Regions to India's Economy

India's economy is a tapestry woven from the diverse contributions of its various regions. Each region of India brings its unique strengths and resources to the nation's economic landscape. From agricultural heartlands to industrial powerhouses and thriving services sectors, the nation's economic diversity is evident in the distinct roles played by different regions. Here's an exploration of the contributions of various regions to India's economy:

1. Northern India:

The northern region, encompassing states like Punjab, Haryana, and Uttar Pradesh, is often referred to as the "food bowl" of India.

It is a major contributor to India's agricultural output, with a focus on wheat, rice, and sugarcane cultivation.

The region also has burgeoning industries and service sectors, with cities like Delhi and Noida serving as economic hubs.

2. Southern India:

Southern states such as Tamil Nadu, Karnataka, and Andhra Pradesh have diverse economies.

They are known for their strong manufacturing sectors, including automobile manufacturing, IT services, and textiles.

The southern region has a significant share in India's software exports and information technology industry.

3. Western India:

Western states like Maharashtra and Gujarat are economic powerhouses.

Maharashtra, with Mumbai as its financial capital, is a hub for finance, entertainment, and services.

Gujarat is known for its industrialization, particularly in sectors like petrochemicals and textiles.

4. Eastern India:

Eastern states like West Bengal, Odisha, and Bihar have rich agricultural traditions.

The region is also witnessing industrial growth, especially in the manufacturing and mining sectors.

West Bengal has a strong presence in sectors like jute, tea, and manufacturing.

5. Northeastern India:

The northeastern states have diverse economies, with a focus on agriculture, horticulture, and handicrafts.

Tourism is a growing sector, with the region's natural beauty and cultural diversity attracting visitors.

6. Central India:

Central Indian states like Madhya Pradesh and Chhattisgarh are rich in mineral resources.

Mining and manufacturing, including steel production, are significant contributors to the regional economy.

7. Coastal States:

Coastal states like Kerala, Goa, and Andhra Pradesh benefit from their proximity to the sea.

Fishing, tourism, and trade are vital components of their economies.

Kerala has a robust remittance economy due to its large expatriate population.

8. Union Territories:

Union territories like Delhi have unique economic profiles.

Delhi serves as the national capital and has a diverse economy, including government, services, and trade.

Puducherry relies on tourism, agriculture, and manufacturing.

9. Himalayan States:

Himalayan states like Himachal Pradesh and Uttarakhand have economic challenges due to their hilly terrain.

They focus on agriculture, horticulture, and tourism for economic growth.

10. Urban-Rural Mix:

- India's economic landscape is also characterized by an urban-rural divide, with urban areas contributing significantly to economic growth through commerce, services, and industry, while rural areas remain primarily agrarian.

11. Small and Medium Enterprises (SMEs):

- SMEs play a crucial role in India's economy and are distributed across various regions. They contribute significantly to employment and economic activity.

12. Cooperative Movements:

- Cooperative movements in states like Gujarat and Maharashtra have fostered economic development in agriculture and dairy sectors.

India's economic diversity is a source of strength and resilience, providing a platform for balanced growth and development. Recognizing the unique contributions of each region and addressing their specific challenges is essential for achieving the nation's economic goals. The nation's journey toward economic progress is a testament to the belief that "Unity Lies in Diversity," even in the realm of economics, where differences become assets in the pursuit of a prosperous and inclusive future.

# IX. Challenges to Unity in Diversity

India, often celebrated as the world's largest democracy and a testament to the principle that "Unity Lies in Diversity," is a nation defined by its vibrant tapestry of cultures, languages, religions, and traditions. This remarkable diversity has been India's strength, a source of resilience and creativity that has shaped its unique identity on the global stage. Yet, amid this celebration of differences, India faces a complex and ongoing challenge—navigating the delicate balance between unity and diversity.

The story of India's unity in diversity is a journey marked by both triumphs and trials. While the nation's pluralistic ethos and democratic values have fostered a sense of unity, it is not immune to challenges that test the very fabric of its diversity. As we delve into the intricate tapestry of India's unity, we must also confront the threads of discord and tension that occasionally strain the bonds of coexistence.

In this exploration of challenges to unity in diversity in India, we embark on a reflective journey, seeking to understand the complexities that arise in a nation where diversity thrives. We examine historical legacies, contemporary issues, and the dynamics that sometimes challenge the nation's unity:

1. Historical Divisions:

India's long history is marked by various divisions, including those of caste, class, and religious identity.

Historical conflicts and disparities have left indelible marks on the nation's social fabric.

2. Communal Tensions:

Communal tensions between religious communities have occasionally erupted into violence, testing India's commitment to secularism and religious harmony.

3. Linguistic and Regional Disparities:

Linguistic and regional disparities persist, raising concerns about equitable development and the preservation of cultural identities.

4. Caste-Based Discrimination:

The caste system, despite legal prohibitions, continues to influence social dynamics, with marginalized communities facing discrimination and unequal opportunities.

5. Economic Disparities:

Economic disparities between regions and social groups pose challenges to inclusive growth and can lead to social unrest.

6. Identity Politics:

Identity-based politics sometimes exacerbate divisions and prioritize narrow interests over the broader welfare of the nation.

7. Political Fragmentation:

The proliferation of regional and local political parties can lead to fragmented politics, making it challenging to form stable governments at the national level.

8. Security Concerns:

Security threats, both internal and external, can strain national unity and require constant vigilance and cooperation among various states and regions.

9. Resource Allocation:

Disputes over the allocation of resources, such as water and minerals, can arise between states, testing cooperative federalism.

10. Environmental Challenges:

- Environmental issues, such as water scarcity and climate change, can exacerbate tensions over resource management.

India's ability to address these challenges and preserve its unity in diversity is a testament to its commitment to democratic principles, pluralism, and the rule of law. The nation's journey is one of continuous self-reflection and adaptation, a reminder that the celebration of diversity is not without its complexities and responsibilities.

In navigating these challenges, India seeks to uphold the fundamental belief that unity is not the absence of diversity but the ability to embrace and respect differences. It is an enduring commitment to the idea that "Unity Lies in Diversity," and that the richness of cultures, traditions, and beliefs can coexist and thrive within the framework of a united and inclusive nation. The challenges to unity in diversity are the crucible in which India's national identity is forged, and the nation's resilience in the face of these challenges continues to shape its remarkable journey.

# A. Communal Tensions and Religious Conflicts in India

Communal tensions and religious conflicts have, at times, posed significant challenges to India's unity in diversity. While India is known for its religious pluralism and a long history of coexistence among diverse religious communities, it has also witnessed instances of religious strife and communal violence. These tensions arise from a complex interplay of historical, social, and political factors. Here's an exploration of communal tensions and religious conflicts in India:

1. Historical Context:

India's history includes periods of religious pluralism and syncretism, where multiple religions and cultures coexisted peacefully. However, it also includes instances of religious conflicts, such as invasions, conquests, and temple destruction.

Historical grievances and memories can sometimes fuel contemporary tensions.

2. Religious Diversity:

India is home to major religions, including Hinduism, Islam, Christianity, Sikhism, Buddhism, Jainism, and others. This diversity can sometimes lead to competition or misunderstandings.

Local variations in religious practices and beliefs can also contribute to tensions.

3. Politicization of Religion:

Politicians and political parties have, at times, exploited religious sentiments for electoral gains, contributing to communal polarization.

The use of religious symbolism and identity in politics can deepen divides.

4. Social and Economic Factors:

Communal tensions can be exacerbated by socio-economic disparities, as marginalized communities may feel marginalized on religious grounds as well.

Economic competition and resource allocation can also lead to religious conflicts.

5. Religious Places and Symbols:

Disputes over religious places, such as temples and mosques, have historically led to conflicts.

These disputes often have legal and political dimensions.

6. Communal Violence:

Communal violence, including riots and clashes between religious communities, has occurred in different parts of India.

Such incidents often result in loss of life and property and can have long-lasting social repercussions.

7. Legal Framework:

India has laws and constitutional provisions aimed at preventing and addressing religious conflicts, such as the Protection of Civil Rights Act and the Scheduled Castes and Scheduled Tribes (Prevention of Atrocities) Act.

The Indian Constitution guarantees religious freedom and prohibits discrimination based on religion.

8. Interfaith Dialogue:

Interfaith dialogue and initiatives to promote religious harmony play a crucial role in mitigating tensions and fostering understanding among different religious communities.

9. Civil Society and NGOs:

Civil society organizations and non-governmental organizations (NGOs) often work to promote communal harmony, provide relief during crises, and facilitate peace-building efforts.

10. Educational Initiatives:

- Educational institutions and curriculum reforms can promote tolerance, secular values, and respect for religious diversity.

- Encouraging religious literacy and interfaith education is vital.

India's journey toward maintaining unity in diversity in the face of communal tensions and religious conflicts is ongoing. While challenges persist, India's democratic institutions, legal safeguards, and diverse civil society initiatives continue to play a critical role in promoting religious harmony and fostering an inclusive society. The nation's commitment to the principles of secularism and religious pluralism remains central to its identity, reinforcing the belief that diversity is a source of strength and that unity can prevail over division.

# B. Caste-Based Discrimination and Social Inequality in India

Caste-based discrimination and social inequality are complex and deeply entrenched challenges that have persisted in India, often challenging the nation's ideal of unity in diversity. The caste system, a social hierarchy that has existed for centuries, has been a source of division, inequality, and injustice. While significant progress has been made to address these issues, they continue to shape India's social landscape. Here's an exploration of caste-based discrimination and social inequality:

1. The Caste System:

The caste system is a traditional social hierarchy that categorizes individuals into groups based on birth.

It includes thousands of castes and sub-castes, each with its own social status and occupational roles.

2. Discrimination and Untouchability:

Historically, certain castes, often referred to as "Scheduled Castes" or "Dalits," faced severe discrimination and were considered "untouchable."

Untouchability practices included denial of access to public spaces, education, and religious places.

3. Legal and Constitutional Efforts:

Independent India has made significant efforts to address caste-based discrimination.

The Indian Constitution abolishes untouchability and provides for affirmative action measures (reservation) for Scheduled Castes and Scheduled Tribes.

4. Challenges of Implementation:

While laws and policies exist to combat caste-based discrimination, their effective implementation has often been hindered by social resistance and administrative challenges.

There are concerns about the effectiveness of reservation policies in addressing deep-rooted inequalities.

5. Social Mobility:

Social mobility remains a challenge for individuals from marginalized castes.

Access to quality education, employment opportunities, and social acceptance can be hindered by caste-based biases.

6. Inter-Caste Marriages:

Inter-caste marriages continue to face societal resistance in many parts of India.

These marriages can challenge traditional caste boundaries but may also lead to social conflicts.

7. Cultural and Religious Practices:

Certain cultural and religious practices perpetuate caste-based discrimination.

These practices can include social segregation and exclusion.

8. Social and Economic Disparities:

Caste-based disparities extend to economic and social realms, with marginalized communities often facing poverty and lack of access to basic services.

9. Social Movements and Activism:

Social reformers like B.R. Ambedkar and contemporary activists have played pivotal roles in raising awareness about caste-based discrimination and advocating for social justice.

10. Government Initiatives:

- The Indian government has initiated various schemes and programs aimed at the economic and social upliftment of marginalized castes.

11. Changing Attitudes:

- There is a gradual shift in societal attitudes, especially among younger generations, towards greater acceptance and inclusivity.

Addressing caste-based discrimination and social inequality is a complex and evolving process. It requires not only legal and policy measures but also shifts in societal attitudes and a commitment to social justice. The recognition that unity in diversity can only be achieved when every citizen is treated with dignity and afforded equal opportunities is central to India's ongoing efforts to combat these deeply entrenched issues. Despite the challenges, India's progress in addressing caste-based discrimination serves as a testament to the nation's resilience and its enduring belief in the principle that unity is strengthened when diversity is celebrated and social justice is upheld.

# C. Regional Disparities and Separatist Movements in India

Regional disparities and separatist movements have at times posed challenges to India's unity in diversity. India's vast and diverse landscape includes regions with varying levels of development, access to resources, and cultural identities. These disparities, coupled with historical grievances, have occasionally given rise to demands for greater autonomy or even separatist movements. Here's an exploration of regional disparities and separatist movements in India:

1. Regional Disparities:

India's regions vary significantly in terms of economic development, infrastructure, and access to basic services.

Disparities can be observed in income levels, education, healthcare, and industrialization.

2. Historical Context:

Historical factors, including princely states' integration into India post-independence, have contributed to regional disparities.

Some regions have felt marginalized due to historical decisions and resource allocation.

3. Demands for Autonomy:

Certain states and regions have demanded greater autonomy in governance and decision-making.

These demands may be rooted in cultural, linguistic, or historical identities.

4. Separatist Movements:

Some regions, such as Jammu and Kashmir in the past, have witnessed separatist movements seeking full independence or autonomy.

These movements can be driven by political, ethnic, religious, or historical factors.

5. Ethnic and Tribal Regions:

Ethnic and tribal regions, particularly in the northeastern states, often have unique cultural identities and aspirations.

Some groups in these regions have sought greater autonomy to preserve their distinct heritage.

6. Security Concerns:

Separatist movements can pose security challenges, leading to tensions between the central government and regions seeking autonomy.

These tensions may have geopolitical implications.

7. Economic Disparities:

Economic disparities between regions can fuel demands for greater control over resources and development priorities.

States may seek more control over taxation and revenue-sharing mechanisms.

8. Federalism and Governance:

India's federal structure allows for significant regional autonomy, but disputes over the division of powers can arise.

Balancing central and state interests is an ongoing challenge.

9. Cultural Preservation:

Some regions seek greater autonomy to preserve and promote their unique languages, traditions, and cultural practices.

Cultural identity is a key driver in demands for autonomy.

10. Resolution Efforts:

- The Indian government has engaged in negotiations and dialogue with various separatist groups to address their concerns.

- Conflict resolution mechanisms and peace talks are ongoing in some regions.

11. Economic Development Initiatives:

- Development initiatives and special economic packages are often used to address regional disparities and address the root causes of separatist movements.

12. National Integration Efforts:

- National integration programs aim to foster a sense of belonging and unity among diverse regions and communities.

India's journey towards maintaining unity in diversity in the face of regional disparities and separatist movements is a dynamic process. While challenges persist, the nation's commitment to addressing grievances, promoting regional development, and upholding the principles of federalism and pluralism remains central to its identity. The belief that unity is strengthened by respecting regional diversity and addressing legitimate aspirations is fundamental to India's ongoing efforts to find common ground and foster inclusivity within its diverse mosaic.

# X. Measures to Promote Unity in Diversity

India, a land celebrated for its cultural kaleidoscope, linguistic tapestry, and religious pluralism, stands as a living testament to the profound principle that "Unity Lies in Diversity." This grand nation, comprising over a billion people, encompasses a multitude of cultures, languages, religions, and traditions, creating a rich mosaic of identities and beliefs. Yet, amid this diversity, India has always recognized the importance of fostering unity, and it continually strives to promote harmony, understanding, and inclusivity among its citizens.

The story of India's unity in diversity is not merely one of coexistence but also a narrative of proactive measures, policies, and collective endeavors aimed at strengthening the bonds that hold this diverse nation together. These measures reflect a commitment to the idea that diversity is not a challenge to unity but an essential source of strength, enrichment, and resilience.

In this exploration of measures to promote unity in diversity in India, we embark on a journey that unveils the deliberate actions taken to harmonize the nation's varied cultural, linguistic, religious, and social dimensions. We delve into the strategies and initiatives that reaffirm India's belief in the principle that "Unity Lies in Diversity."

1. Constitutional Guarantees:

India's Constitution enshrines principles of secularism, equality, and religious freedom.

It prohibits discrimination on the grounds of religion, caste, gender, or place of birth.

2. Affirmative Action and Reservations:

Affirmative action policies, including reservations in education and government jobs, aim to uplift marginalized and disadvantaged communities, particularly Scheduled Castes, Scheduled Tribes, and Other Backward Classes.

3. Cultural Preservation:

The preservation and promotion of diverse cultural heritage through initiatives like cultural festivals, museums, and historical preservation sites celebrate India's rich tapestry of traditions.

4. Multilingualism and Language Policies:

India recognizes multiple languages and has adopted a policy of multilingualism.

It promotes linguistic diversity while ensuring the use of Hindi and English as link languages.

5. Interfaith Dialogue:

Interfaith dialogue and harmony initiatives promote understanding and peaceful coexistence among religious communities.

6. Education and Awareness:

Educational programs and curricula promote diversity, tolerance, and inclusivity.

These initiatives encourage students to appreciate and respect different cultures and traditions.

7. Social Reforms:

Social reform movements, led by visionaries like Mahatma Gandhi and B.R. Ambedkar, have challenged discriminatory practices and fostered inclusivity.

8. Civil Society and NGOs:

Civil society organizations and non-governmental organizations work tirelessly to address social disparities, promote communal harmony, and advocate for marginalized communities.

9. Federalism and Decentralization:

India's federal structure empowers states and regions, allowing them to address local needs and foster a sense of regional identity.

10. Inclusive Governance:

- Inclusive governance practices involve citizens from diverse backgrounds in decision-making processes.

- Representation of marginalized communities in elected bodies is actively encouraged.

11. National Integration Programs:

- National integration programs aim to promote unity and harmony across different states and regions.

12. Grassroots Initiatives:

- Local community-driven initiatives and grassroots movements play a pivotal role in fostering unity and diversity at the grassroots level.

India's commitment to unity in diversity is an enduring belief that transcends geographical, cultural, and religious boundaries. It is a belief that the nation's strength lies not in uniformity but in its ability to embrace and celebrate differences. The measures taken to promote unity in diversity are a testament to India's resilience, adaptability, and its unwavering dedication to the idea that diversity is not a challenge to be overcome but a source of enrichment and strength that binds the nation together in its shared journey.

# A. Educational Initiatives to Foster Tolerance and Inclusivity in India

Education plays a pivotal role in fostering tolerance, inclusivity, and a sense of unity in diversity in India. Recognizing the transformative power of education, the Indian government and various organizations have implemented a range of initiatives to promote these values. These educational initiatives aim to create a more harmonious and inclusive society by instilling respect for diversity and promoting social cohesion. Here's an exploration of some of these initiatives:

1. Inclusive Curriculum:

The Indian education system emphasizes the development of curricula that celebrate India's diverse cultural heritage, languages, and traditions.

Curricular materials often include content that promotes tolerance, secularism, and respect for all religions and communities.

2. Moral and Value Education:

Moral and value education is integrated into the curriculum to impart ethical values, empathy, and respect for diversity.

These programs teach students the importance of tolerance, non-violence, and inclusivity.

3. Awareness Campaigns:

Educational institutions, along with government and non-governmental organizations, conduct awareness campaigns on issues related to communal harmony, gender equality, and social justice.

These campaigns often involve workshops, seminars, and interactive sessions with experts.

4. History and Civics Education:

History and civics textbooks are designed to provide a balanced and inclusive view of India's historical and political journey.

They highlight the contributions of various communities and leaders to the nation's development.

5. Interfaith Dialogue Programs:

Schools and colleges organize interfaith dialogues and seminars to promote understanding among students from different religious backgrounds.

These initiatives encourage open discussions on religious diversity and coexistence.

6. Multilingual Education:

Multilingual education policies acknowledge the linguistic diversity in India.

They aim to preserve and promote regional languages while ensuring proficiency in Hindi and English as link languages.

7. Scholarships and Affirmative Action:

Scholarships and affirmative action programs promote educational access for marginalized communities, including Scheduled Castes, Scheduled Tribes, and Other Backward Classes.

These initiatives reduce educational disparities and foster inclusivity.

8. Student Exchanges and Cultural Programs:

Student exchange programs and cultural events provide opportunities for students to interact with peers from diverse backgrounds.

These programs promote cross-cultural understanding and friendships.

9. Social Studies and Citizenship Education:

Social studies and citizenship education focus on building responsible citizens who respect diversity and uphold democratic values.

Students learn about their rights and responsibilities as citizens.

10. Sensitization Workshops:

- Sensitization workshops for teachers and school staff equip them with the knowledge and skills to create inclusive and tolerant learning environments.

- These workshops address biases and prejudices.

11. Diversity Clubs and Student Organizations:

- Many educational institutions have diversity clubs and student organizations that organize cultural events, discussions, and community service projects.

- These groups promote diversity awareness on campuses.

12. Online Resources:

- Educational websites and digital resources provide information on diversity, tolerance, and inclusivity.

- Online platforms facilitate discussions and awareness campaigns.

These educational initiatives underscore India's commitment to fostering a sense of unity in diversity from an early age. By instilling values of tolerance, inclusivity, and respect for all, the education system plays a vital role in shaping the future of the nation. It reflects India's belief that true unity is achieved not by suppressing diversity but by celebrating and respecting it, ensuring that every citizen can contribute to the nation's progress while retaining their unique identities and cultures.

# B. Government Policies to Promote Cultural Exchange and Understanding in India

Cultural exchange and understanding are vital components of India's efforts to foster unity in diversity. The Indian government recognizes the importance of promoting cultural exchanges and interactions as a means to celebrate the nation's rich diversity and strengthen social cohesion. Various policies and initiatives have been implemented to facilitate cultural exchange and promote understanding among different communities. Here's an exploration of some of these government policies:

1. National Cultural Policy:

India has articulated a National Cultural Policy to preserve, protect, and promote the diverse cultural heritage of the nation.

This policy seeks to encourage cultural exchanges and collaborations among different communities and regions.

2. Cultural Festivals and Events:

The government supports and sponsors cultural festivals and events that showcase the traditions, music, dance, and art forms of various communities.

These events often involve participation from artists and performers across the country.

3. Heritage Preservation and Promotion:

The Archaeological Survey of India (ASI) and other agencies work to preserve and promote historical and cultural heritage sites.

Efforts are made to ensure that these sites are accessible to people from all backgrounds.

4. Promotion of Traditional Arts:

Various government schemes and initiatives support traditional arts and crafts, such as handloom and handicrafts.

These programs aim to preserve traditional skills and promote the economic well-being of artisans.

5. Cultural Exchange Programs:

India actively participates in international cultural exchange programs and collaborations with other nations.

These programs facilitate cultural diplomacy and strengthen ties with other countries.

6. Museums and Cultural Centers:

Museums and cultural centers funded by the government house artifacts and exhibits representing India's diverse cultural heritage.

These institutions educate visitors about the nation's pluralistic identity.

7. Promotion of Regional Languages:

The government promotes the use and preservation of regional languages and dialects, recognizing their cultural significance.

Literary events and language promotion programs are organized.

8. Scholarships and Grants:

Scholarships and grants are awarded to artists, scholars, and researchers to conduct studies and projects related to India's cultural diversity.

These initiatives encourage research and documentation of cultural practices.

9. Cultural Diplomacy:

Indian embassies and cultural centers abroad actively engage in cultural diplomacy, organizing exhibitions, performances, and cultural events to showcase Indian diversity.

10. Cultural Exchange with States:

- India's federal structure allows states to promote their unique cultural identities.

- State governments often organize cultural exchange programs and festivals.

11. Educational Initiatives:

- Educational institutions receive support to include cultural studies and diversity awareness in their curricula.

- Cultural exchange programs for students promote cross-cultural understanding.

12. Promotion of Traditional Music and Dance:

- The government supports traditional music and dance forms through festivals, competitions, and training programs.

- These initiatives preserve and promote cultural expressions.

These government policies and initiatives underscore India's commitment to celebrating its diverse cultural heritage and promoting unity through cultural exchange and understanding. By actively encouraging interactions among different communities and regions, India aims to build bridges of understanding and strengthen the fabric of its pluralistic society. The belief that cultural diversity is an asset that enriches the nation's identity and contributes to its unity remains at the heart of these policies.

# C. Grassroots Efforts to Bridge Divides in India

In addition to government policies and educational initiatives, grassroots efforts play a crucial role in bridging divides and promoting unity in diversity in India. These community-driven initiatives, often led by individuals, non-governmental organizations (NGOs), and civil society groups, are at the forefront of efforts to foster understanding, tolerance, and inclusivity. Here's an exploration of some of the grassroots efforts in India:

1. Interfaith Dialogue and Harmony Groups:

Interfaith dialogue forums and community-led harmony groups bring together individuals from different religious backgrounds.

These groups facilitate open discussions, cultural exchanges, and joint celebrations of festivals.

2. Communal Harmony Campaigns:

Grassroots organizations and community leaders organize campaigns and events that promote communal harmony and peace, particularly in areas prone to religious tensions.

3. Women's Self-Help Groups:

Women's self-help groups provide a platform for women from diverse backgrounds to come together, share experiences, and work towards economic empowerment.

These groups often transcend caste, religion, and class divisions.

4. Village-level Initiatives:

In rural areas, local community leaders and organizations work to resolve disputes and conflicts, emphasizing peaceful coexistence.

These initiatives address issues related to land disputes, water resources, and communal tensions.

5. Cultural Exchanges and Festivals:

Grassroots efforts often involve organizing cultural exchange programs, festivals, and performances that showcase the traditions and talents of various communities.

These events provide opportunities for people to learn about and appreciate diverse cultures.

6. Youth Engagement Programs:

Youth-led organizations and programs focus on promoting understanding and tolerance among the younger generation.

These initiatives include workshops, seminars, and community service projects.

7. Human Rights and Social Justice Advocacy:

Grassroots organizations advocate for the rights of marginalized and oppressed communities, working to eliminate discrimination and injustice.

They often engage in legal activism and awareness campaigns.

8. Educational Initiatives in Rural Areas:

NGOs and volunteers establish informal schools and educational centers in underserved rural areas.

These initiatives provide access to education for children from marginalized communities.

9. Grassroots Media:

Local newspapers, community radio stations, and digital platforms operated by grassroots organizations promote stories of unity, diversity, and social inclusivity.

10. Community-Based Healthcare Programs:

- Healthcare initiatives at the grassroots level often focus on underserved communities and promote health equity regardless of caste, religion, or economic status.

11. Environmental Conservation Projects:

- Grassroots environmental organizations often involve communities in conservation efforts, fostering a sense of shared responsibility and unity.

12. Neighborhood Associations:

- Neighborhood associations work to create inclusive and harmonious communities where people from various backgrounds live together peacefully.

These grassroots efforts are driven by the belief that real change starts at the local level, within communities, and among individuals. They emphasize the values of compassion, empathy, and respect for diversity. By addressing social, cultural, and economic divides through these initiatives, grassroots organizations and individuals contribute significantly to India's ongoing journey towards unity in diversity. These efforts reinforce the idea that every citizen, regardless of their background, can play a role in building a more inclusive and harmonious society.

# XI. Conclusion

India, a land of myriad cultures, languages, religions, and traditions, stands as a beacon of unity in diversity. Throughout its history and into the present day, India has demonstrated an unwavering commitment to the principle that diversity is not a source of division but a wellspring of strength and enrichment. The nation's journey toward fostering unity in the midst of this remarkable diversity is a testament to its resilience, adaptability, and enduring belief in the values of tolerance, inclusivity, and social harmony.

From the ancient civilizations that flourished on its soil to the modern democratic nation it has become, India's historical tapestry is woven with threads of diversity. This diversity is evident in the multitude of languages spoken, the rich tapestry of religions practiced, the colorful array of festivals celebrated, and the myriad regional and ethnic identities that coexist within its borders.

India's commitment to unity in diversity is embedded in its Constitution, which enshrines the principles of secularism, equality, and religious freedom. Government policies and educational initiatives actively promote cultural exchanges, interfaith dialogue, and social justice, fostering an environment where diversity is cherished and respected.

At the grassroots level, countless individuals, community leaders, NGOs, and civil society groups work tirelessly to bridge divides, promote communal harmony, and advocate for the rights of marginalized communities. These efforts serve as a reminder that unity is not a top-down imposition but a bottom-up aspiration that thrives in the hearts and actions of everyday citizens.

As India navigates the challenges that arise from its diversity, including communal tensions, caste-based discrimination, regional disparities, and separatist movements, it remains steadfast in its commitment to finding common ground and embracing differences. It recognizes that the path to unity may be fraught with complexities, but it is a path worth traveling.

In conclusion, India's journey of "Unity Lies in Diversity" is a testament to the enduring belief that diversity is an asset, not a liability. It is a source of resilience and creativity that has shaped India's unique identity on the global stage. As the nation continues to celebrate its rich tapestry of cultures and traditions, it reaffirms its commitment to fostering unity, inclusivity, and social cohesion. The challenges it faces only serve to strengthen its resolve to uphold the principles of tolerance, pluralism, and the profound belief that diversity is, and will always be, the cornerstone of India's strength and identity.

# A. Reiteration of the importance of "Unity in Diversity" in India

In concluding the exploration of "Unity in Diversity" in India, it is imperative to reiterate the profound significance of this principle in the nation's identity and journey. India, as a diverse and pluralistic nation, embodies the essence that unity is not merely the absence of differences but the celebration of those differences. This celebration is not a passive act but a proactive commitment to understanding, tolerance, and inclusivity.

The importance of "Unity in Diversity" in India lies at the very heart of its existence and progress. It is through the harmonious coexistence of countless cultures, languages, and traditions that India has not only preserved its rich heritage but also thrived as a dynamic and resilient nation.

Strength Through Diversity: India's diverse populace contributes to the nation's strength and adaptability. It is a source of creativity, innovation, and cultural richness. India's diverse talent pool has made significant contributions to various fields, including science, art, literature, and technology.

Resilience in the Face of Challenges: India's history has been marked by a multitude of challenges, yet it has consistently demonstrated resilience and unity in the face of adversity. It is the diverse tapestry of the nation that fortifies its capacity to navigate complex issues and emerge stronger.

Global Influence: India's commitment to "Unity in Diversity" has garnered international recognition. The nation's soft power, including its cultural exports, philosophical teachings, and diplomatic engagements, reflects its reputation as a beacon of pluralism and peaceful coexistence.

Safeguarding Democracy: The democratic values enshrined in India's Constitution thrive in an environment where diverse voices are heard and respected. The principle of secularism ensures that all citizens have equal rights and opportunities regardless of their backgrounds.

Role Model for the World: India's journey toward unity in diversity serves as a source of inspiration for nations grappling with their own diversity-related challenges. It showcases that differences need not be divisive but can be the catalyst for progress and mutual enrichment.

A Moral Imperative: Beyond its practical benefits, "Unity in Diversity" in India is a moral imperative, reflecting the nation's commitment to justice, equality, and human rights. It underscores the belief that every individual, regardless of their background, deserves dignity and respect.

In India's ongoing narrative, the principle of "Unity in Diversity" is not an abstract ideal but a lived reality. It is witnessed in the bustling markets of its cities, the tranquil villages of its countryside, the myriad languages spoken, the places of worship where diverse faiths come together, and the celebrations of festivals that transcend religious and regional boundaries.

As India continues to navigate the complexities of a rapidly changing world, it stands firm in its belief that unity is strengthened by embracing diversity. It is a belief that echoes not only in India's national identity but in its aspirations for a harmonious and inclusive society, where every citizen finds a sense of belonging and contributes to the nation's progress.

In sum, "Unity in Diversity" in India is not just a slogan but a guiding principle that defines the nation's essence. It is a philosophy that serves as a reminder to the world that diversity is not a challenge to be overcome but a treasure to be celebrated. India's enduring commitment to this principle reaffirms its place as a shining example of how unity can truly flourish amidst the beautiful tapestry of diversity.

# B. Reflection on India's potential as a role model for the world

India's Potential as a Role Model for the World

India's journey of "Unity in Diversity" presents a compelling case for its potential as a role model for the world. This diverse nation, with its complex tapestry of cultures, languages, religions, and traditions, offers valuable lessons and inspiration to nations grappling with issues related to diversity, inclusion, and social cohesion. Here's a reflection on India's potential as a global role model:

Celebration of Pluralism: India's ability to celebrate its pluralism sets an example for nations facing identity-based conflicts. India's mosaic of identities, rather than being a source of division, is celebrated as a source of strength. It demonstrates that a nation can thrive when it values and respects the diversity of its people.

Democratic Values: India's commitment to democracy, secularism, and religious freedom is a beacon of hope for countries striving to strike a balance between diverse faiths and governance. India's democratic institutions and processes showcase the importance of respecting individual rights and freedoms.

Soft Power and Cultural Diplomacy: India's soft power, including its art, literature, cinema, and yoga, has gained global recognition. Its ability to project cultural influence while respecting diverse traditions serves as a model for cultural diplomacy in a globalized world.

Peaceful Coexistence of Religions: India's history is a testament to the peaceful coexistence of major religions such as Hinduism, Islam, Christianity, Sikhism, Buddhism, and Jainism. It demonstrates that different faiths can thrive side by side when there is tolerance, respect, and dialogue.

Striving for Social Justice: India's efforts to address historical injustices, such as caste-based discrimination and social inequality, reflect its commitment to social justice. This journey of rectifying historical wrongs serves as an inspiration for nations grappling with similar issues.

Economic and Technological Advancement: India's rapid economic growth and technological prowess showcase that a diverse population can contribute to innovation and development. It serves as a model for harnessing human capital to drive economic progress.

Global Multilingualism: India's multilingual society, where citizens often speak multiple languages, exemplifies the possibilities and benefits of multilingualism. It highlights the importance of language preservation and the potential for coexistence of multiple languages.

Sustainable Practices: India's traditional practices, including yoga, Ayurveda, and sustainable agriculture, offer valuable lessons for sustainable living and well-being. These practices align with global efforts towards sustainable development.

Peaceful Resolution of Conflicts: India's commitment to dialogue and peaceful conflict resolution is evident in its diplomacy with neighboring countries. It sets an example for resolving disputes through dialogue and diplomacy rather than confrontation.

Global Diaspora: The Indian diaspora, with its significant presence around the world, serves as a bridge between India and other nations. It exemplifies how diverse communities can integrate and contribute positively to their host countries.

International Cooperation: India's active participation in international organizations and its commitment to global challenges such as climate change and public health issues demonstrate its role as a responsible global citizen.

Resilience in the Face of Challenges: India's ability to navigate complex challenges while maintaining its commitment to diversity and unity is a testament to its resilience and adaptability.

While India's journey towards unity in diversity is far from perfect, its ongoing efforts to uphold these principles and address challenges are a source of inspiration. India's potential as a role model for the world lies not in claiming to have all the answers but in its willingness to learn, adapt, and work towards a more harmonious and inclusive society. As the world continues to grapple with issues related to diversity, India's experiences and lessons can serve as a guidepost towards a more inclusive and interconnected future.

# C. Call to embrace and celebrate diversity while striving for unity

In this age of globalization and interconnectedness, the call to embrace and celebrate diversity while striving for unity is more vital than ever. India, with its rich history and diverse tapestry of cultures, languages, religions, and traditions, serves as an inspiring example of how a nation can flourish when it values and respects the differences among its people. This call transcends borders and holds relevance for societies worldwide. Here is a heartfelt appeal to embrace and celebrate diversity while pursuing unity:

1. Celebrate the Mosaic of Humanity:

Let us recognize that the world is a tapestry woven with the threads of countless cultures, each adding its unique color and texture. Our differences are not obstacles; they are the building blocks of our collective heritage.

2. Promote Inclusivity:

Embrace the notion that unity is not homogeneity. Inclusivity means creating spaces where everyone, regardless of their background, feels welcomed and valued. It means ensuring that no one is left behind.

3. Empathy and Understanding:

Strive to understand the experiences, perspectives, and challenges of those who are different from us. Empathy is the bridge that connects hearts and fosters genuine connections.

4. Cultural Exchange and Learning:

Actively engage in cultural exchange, dialogue, and learning. There is immense beauty in discovering the traditions, languages, and beliefs of others. It broadens our horizons and enriches our lives.

5. Respect for All Faiths:

Let us respect the diversity of religious beliefs and practices. Religion should be a source of inspiration, compassion, and love, not division or hatred.

6. Equity and Justice:

Advocate for equity and justice in all aspects of life. Acknowledge that historical injustices must be rectified, and systemic inequalities addressed for true unity to flourish.

7. Peaceful Resolution of Conflicts:

Commit to peaceful dialogue and diplomacy as the means to resolve conflicts, both domestic and international. The world can be a better place when differences are resolved through understanding rather than violence.

8. Embrace Multilingualism:

Multilingualism is a testament to human ingenuity. Let us celebrate the richness of languages and promote linguistic diversity as a source of connection.

9. Environmental Stewardship:

Recognize that preserving the environment is a collective responsibility. Embrace diverse practices and traditional wisdom that contribute to sustainable living.

10. Celebrate the Human Spirit:

Ultimately, our shared humanity is what binds us together. Celebrate the human spirit's resilience, creativity, and capacity for compassion.

11. Educate and Inspire:

Teach the next generation the value of diversity and the importance of unity. Inspire them to be global citizens who respect and celebrate differences.

12. Lead by Example:

Let us lead by example in our communities, workplaces, and nations. Our actions can inspire change and demonstrate that unity in diversity is not an abstract ideal but a lived reality.

In a world where division and intolerance can threaten peace and progress, embracing and celebrating diversity while striving for unity is a noble aspiration. It is a call to rise above prejudices, biases, and fears and to recognize that, despite our differences, we are all part of the same human family. As India has shown, unity is not achieved by erasing diversity but by cherishing it. In diversity, we find our collective strength, resilience, and the boundless potential to create a brighter, more inclusive world for generations to come.

# Also by Swatantra Bahadur

Breaking Barriers: LGBTQ Rights and Social Justice
Blossom with confidence
"Depression: A Roller Coaster Ride"
Finding Your Voice
Rahul Gandhi: The Untold Story
100 Aspects on Nature
Love By An Introvert
Man Of Golden India "Narendra Modi"
India " Unity lies in Diversity"
Indian's Heritage of Kashi "Varanasi"

# Also by Mahima Tripathi

India " Unity lies in Diversity"

# About the Author

Instagram Id - swatantrabahadur15

www.ingramcontent.com/pod-product-compliance
Lightning Source LLC
Chambersburg PA
CBHW071327130726
47996CB00002B/655